I0460672

Fire in the Snow

Book One of the Calypto Cycle

The Calypto Cycle

Fire in the Snow
Shackles of Doubt (forthcoming in 2017)

Fire in the Snow

D. Thomas Minton

This novel is a work of fiction. All character, places, and incidents describe herein are fictitious. Any resemblance to actual events, places or persons is entirely coincidental.

Copyright © 2017 D. Thomas Minton
Cover art by Hans Binder Knott © 2016
Cover design by Holly Heisey

No part of this publication may be reproduced or transmitted, in any form by any means, except by an authorized retailer, or with written permission of the author.

This book is available in print and electronic formats and at most online retailers.

ISBN: 0998304204
ISBN-13: 978-0-9983042-0-5

This one is for Mom & Dad

PART I

MISSION FILE: CLASS-A

今

WE ALL HAVE TALENTS, some more useful than others–feline grace, gifts with complex numbers, the ability to see the future. Well, I don't exactly *see* the future. More than anything, it's a feeling of things out of alignment. Things dangerously wrong. It's as if the fabric of reality has momentarily snagged on something sharp, stopping its smooth flow forward before tearing free and lurching back to where it should be. When that happens, I've learned to duck because the world is a bitch when it snaps back.

I scamper for cover behind a stoop with a wrought iron railing, and scan the street for danger. The sun has not yet peeked over the stone buildings huddling together to share warmth. Stoops, like the one I hide behind, dot the tenements at regular intervals like punctuation. On the opposite side, a woman in a battered coat flickers between a line of autos nudged up against the curb.

The click of an old man's cane stops as he pauses to squint at me in the shadows. "Don't think I don't see you," he says with a gravelly voice. Then he

1

mutters, "Rapscallions," as he lowers his head into the east wind and continues, the worn brass cane tip clicking on the ice along the edge of the sidewalk.

I must look the part, skulking in shadows and coal soot. My long coat has seen a dozen winters and a thousand miles, and no doubt looks it. My scraggly beard—a comfort on heatless mornings—gives me the face of a desperate man. There are a lot of desperate men in the Empire these days because these are desperate times, with the war and the shortages. Even here in the Empire's capital, mighty Aurestapol, sacrifices have been made.

The whirring of a flywheel engine bounces off the buildings as an auto turns out of an alley. The vehicle's sun visors are lowered even though the light through the coal smoke and winter cloud pack is watery and dim. Shielded by the visors are stern, mustached faces, dark coated shoulders. The driver's black-gloved hands wrap tightly around the wheel.

A government auto, and from the look of the two men in the front, it's a dignitary and his bodyguards.

An odd hour for an official of the Empire to be on the road. That can only mean his movement is intended to be unexpected, which suggests the occupant is concerned for his safety, not that anyone is truly safe these days. Two days ago, Papalate spies derailed a commuter train, killing nineteen. Or so says word on the street. The Empire's official news agency doesn't report such things, so news like that stays compartmentalized and travels slowly across the vast Empire.

I scan the buildings, for something out of place. The windows are dark, save an odd one here or there flickering softly with candlelight because the power grid in this section of the city won't come online for another hour. In an alley across the street, a fire escape's ladder is pulled down–an oversight of a teen who has snuck off to raise hell with his friends or something sinister?

The metal ladders zigzag up the side of the tenement, but there is nothing else to see. My vision slides along the edge of the roof and stops at a pinprick of light glinting through a scupper. Barely visible in the gray light is the black barrel of a flechette rifle, like a faint scratch on a photograph.

The whir of the engine drops an octave as the government auto rolls past me.

No shiver of precognition, but I know in an instant, everything will be over.

I sprint across the street, dashing full speed into the cover of the buildings. Here the shooter has no angle on me, but I'm not the one he wants, or I would probably already be dead. I catch the rung of the fire escape ladder as glass explodes on the street behind me. The auto swerves and tries to accelerate away. Flechettes whistle through the air, the heavy hum of large-caliber ammunition. A tire blows out and more glass shatters. The auto squeals and, from the sound of it, has careened off the road into a stoop.

I make the first landing and draw my FP from its holster under my long coat. The winter air is a shock against my chest, but the pistol is body-warm and fits snugly into my palm like an old friend. I zigzag up the ladders; each time I come around to face the street, I look for the government car, but see nothing. The street remains quiet, even though the crash was loud. People are afraid to come out. I can't blame them; I wouldn't come out if I were in their place. The curious quickly become the dead.

That thought makes me pause at the base of the last ladder up to the edge of the roof. I don't know what I'm running into, and if I don't slow down, I'll find myself perforated. I take the last ladder slowly, my FP ready, my eyes stitched to the roofline. As my head comes nearly level with the rooftop, a leg with the diameter of spruce comes over the short retaining wall, dragging behind it a man the size of bear.

I drop immediately into a crouch, bracing myself on the step.

He sees me, and in that instant, his features flash by—a square face, flat as a plank. A nose that looks like a flattened fungus. Heavy lips in the middle of a thick black mustache and beard. Small eyes, earthy brown, huddled beneath equally thick eyebrows.

I fire.

The stream of flechettes misses, and the bear man is on me. He smashes hard into my chest. The force of his blow nearly knocks me over the railing, and jars my FP from my grip. It clatters onto the landing below me. My feet come up off the metal, and for a second I think it's over for me, but my flailing hand catches the bear man's coat by the back of its collar, and I don't take a three-story tumble. Instead I'm dragged across the landing, my weight pulling at his coat. I tumble to the metal grating as he slips out of the coat and bounds down the fire escape in thunderous leaps.

I don't know how I missed.

No, I do. In an eye blink he had come over the wall and smashed me against the railing, my flechettes whistling through the empty air where he had been.

Somehow, he had bent his body enough to avoid the stream of metal that should have perforated his chest and neck.

Damn he's fast. Unnaturally fast.

Already bear man has reached the bottom landing, and is climbing over the railing. Without his coat, I see how big he really is—his torso is a barrel that stretches his sleeveless undershirt tight as a drum head across his back. He drops into the alley where he lands in a crouch. He doesn't straighten, but explodes forward like a sprinter leaving the starting block. As he straightens, I see a black mark on his neck. It barely registers in my mind because I'm busy hustling down to my weapon. By the time I retrieve it, the bear man has sprinted the length of the alley, and turned out of sight down another street.

The echo of his soft shoes has faded except in my head. It's as if my mind refuses to believe it's gone. So fast—I've never seen someone so fast.

An eerie silence settles over Aurestapol, like mustard gas on the front. Only seconds have passed since the government auto crashed. If no one survived the crash, I expect to hear nothing for a long while.

On the roof, the black tar has already warmed enough to melt the ice into dark patches like sweat stains. Faint wisps of coal smoke trickles from u-vents, smelling like prosperity.

Near the retaining wall facing the street, I find the assassin's rifle—an Avignon 750 with an external compression canister for extra power, a model favored by Papalate snipers. I've seen pictures of it, and thankfully have never been on the wrong end of one; it's claimed many Empire lives across the no man's land of the Romani front.

In the street below, the black-gloved driver slumps over the auto's steering wheel. The shattered windshield has a splatter of red on it. The government man from the passenger side has stumbled out on to the sidewalk and crouches on his hands and knees. He is injured but looks like he will live. The window on the rear door is shattered and small flechette holes pepper the side of the vehicle.

I duck back when the government man starts to raise his head in my direction. He will get his wits about him soon, and when he does, he will come up here. I can't afford entanglements, so I retreat from the roof. There is nothing I can do, anyhow.

My boots land softly in the alley, and I'm gone long before anyone comes to investigate.

今

Even at this early hour, the lobby of Aurestapol's Grand Station is alive with activity. Soldiers in their winter browns shift nervously as they prepare to head to the western fronts or duty stations in the east. They file in long lines down the stairs from the lobby to troop carriers lining platforms that stretch outward below like splayed fingers. Standing tall in the middle of everything, the Armistice Clock ticks off the seconds of existence. It was a gift of friendship sixty years ago from the people we now fight. Above, the dome, gilded with gold and inlaid with precious stones, sweeps to heights unimagined. Other than the spires of the White Palace and the bell tower on St. Demetrius, it's the tallest building in the city. It can be seen from anywhere in Aurestapol, a symbol of our technological superiority.

Or at least that's what we like to think. I've been to Roma and seen the Plaza di Cristo and the great palaces of worship with their walls of stained glass windows and doors so large and ornate they must open onto their heaven itself, because to open into

7

any other mundane place would be wrong. We are more evenly matched than our leaders would like anyone to believe, even if the proof is obvious on the battlefield.

I pass soldiers speaking in whispers. They know where they head, and the dangers they will face. While most will undoubtedly come home, many will not, and they know this, too. Even though their individual voices are quiet, their collective din rises as a rumble into the dome overhead, creating a cacophony that rings in my ears.

R sits at a table in the only open café. The roundness of her face and her dark hair streaked with silver pulled up into a bun under a headscarf look out of place among the stern officers that fill the café's other tables. I wonder how she got a place here; we are not military, and they seem to own the Grand Station this morning.

R sees me as I emerge from the sea of brown. She sets down her drink, but makes no other motion to indicate she knows me.

"You're late, Calypto," she says, as I sit down across from her.

"There was an assassination attempt near the Citadel," I say.

R makes an unimpressed humph as if such things are everyday occurrences, which thankfully, they are not. The fragrant scent of bergamot and citrus steams from her cup. Next to it on the table is a brown manila envelope looped shut with a red string, but otherwise featureless. R's pudgy hand moves protectively atop of it, as if she's afraid I will try to take it.

"I don't know who," I say. "A government official

by the looks of the vehicle."

"Is he dead?"

"I didn't stick around to find out, but the shooter—"

"Papalate," R says. It's not a question.

I shrug. I saw the gun, yes. The man's features, yes. All point to the Papalate, but that's only one thing that makes me suspicious.

"You don't agree?" she asks.

"He was fast. Talent-fast."

R sits forward in her chair and fixes her gaze on me. She has beautiful eyes. Frightening, but beautiful. I both love it and hate it when they pierce into me. If our relationship hadn't been what it was, I might have found her attractive, even if she is twenty years my senior. Time has been kind to her, or perhaps is afraid to cross her.

"We don't have a monopoly on talent," she says. "But that *is* interesting."

"It's more than that, too," I say. "He left the weapon behind."

"You surprised him."

"He left it before he saw me. He intended to leave it like he wanted us to find it."

"Maybe he intends to walk out, and couldn't take it with him."

Possible, I have to concede. If he expected to walk away, carrying an Avignon 750 wouldn't be easy. People would ask questions, and the ears of the Red Cuffs are everywhere, even here, I'm sure. As sure as the Armistice Clock will strike six at any moment.

Yet I can't shake the feeling that there is something more to this assassin.

"He had a tattoo on his neck," I say, pulling the memory up from somewhere deep. The mark was out

9

of place–something I've not seen before–and not something I'd expect to see on a Papalate soldier because to mark the body is to mark the temple of God, or so they believe. "It looked like this." With my finger, I draw an inverted vee on the table and a horizontal line inside of it. Then under it, I draw two more lines connected to form a right angle. It looks a little like a house that a child would draw.

R hands me a pen and taps on the manila envelope. I draw the tattoo again, in glistening black ink and spin it around for her see it right-side up.

Her brow squeezes together in thought, but otherwise I can't read her expression. "Odd for a Papalate assassin to have a body marking," she says, "but not unheard of either."

Maybe the war goes as poorly for them as it does for us, and they have lowered their standards for what they will accept into their ranks. Tattoos are the marks of criminals–cutthroats and killers–the perfect type of men for the meat grinder this conflict has evolved into.

"But right now, it's not your concern," R says when I don't respond in agreement with her. "This is." She slides the envelope across the table. The tattoo glares up at me. "We have a Class-A package that needs pick up in Olesk. Birdie will meet you in the Karakulov Market on Tuesday morning. She will have everything you need."

"That's the day after tomorrow."

She slides a small rectangle of blue paper to me. "A ticket for the next train. It leaves–" she removes a pocket watch, a delicate disc of silver gears and dials encased in a glass plate revealing the inner workings of the machine "–in fifteen minutes."

As she speaks the words, the Armistice Clock chimes the hour, six loud bells. They are melancholy tones that drub my heart.

"Good thing you weren't any later," R says, disapproval in her voice. "The next train after that is tomorrow." She taps the envelope. "Your full instructions are inside." She gently nudges a small shoulder bag from under the table.

I know better than to open the orders here. R demands my full attention, and if I was meant to hear these orders now, R would tell me them and not bother with the paper. I fold the envelope and tuck it into an inner pocket on my long coat. I take the ticket and check the platform.

"Is there anything else?" I ask.

"Be careful, Calypto." For a moment I sense genuine concern in her voice. My work is dangerous, and with each envelope she gives me, there is a chance I will not come back. She must know that too, and distance is generally her defense. She must care for us, but must not care about us. She is my handler, and I know I am nothing but a piece in the vast game orchestrated by The Order for which I work.

Which is why her words unsettle me now. Is there something more she knows that she's not telling me? If so, why is she concealing it? I dismiss that thought as healthy paranoia. R has always been straight with me, and until I experience otherwise, I trust her. I must trust her.

"I'll be careful," I say.

My train slides away from the platform the moment my shoes mount the steps. I pull myself into the car as it picks up speed and approaches the tunnels that will take it from the Grand Station to the world outside. I push my way through the crowded corridors to my assigned compartment. The train is filled with soldiers heading to Olesk. There is concern about the eastern front because the Quin Empire is rumored to be on the verge of an alliance with the Papalate, which has triggered unrest along the border.

My compartment is small, with a simple table, bench and a pull-down bed, but at least it has a private head. The lamp over the table swings gently with the swaying of the car, throwing shadows around the room like cards. I slide the door shut, but it only muffles the boisterousness of the soldiers as they drink and celebrate. If they were heading to one of the western fronts, it would likely be their last celebration for a while, but I don't know what to expect in Olesk.

I tear open the envelope and slide out the single sheet of onionskin, a small stack of paper bills, and a worn billfold. I tuck the money into my pocket without counting it and check the billfold: inside are a set of credentials identifying me as an official of the Bureau of Medicine and Human Services. They are stamped, notarized, and by all accounts authentic. I commit the basic information to memory and tuck the billfold into my pocket. I hope to never need it.

My orders have been typed, heavy letters struck into the paper as if with a hammer and not teletype. Succinct, they consist of only five lines:

> BEGIN TRANS
> Stall 734, Karakulov Market, Olesk
> 17-01, 0900
> Return Class-A, Home 7-ORION, Report
> END TRANS

Class-A. No higher level of importance for a package. I've handled a few of them in the past, from all parts of the world, including from behind Papalate lines. They are Class-A for two reasons: They are extremely important to the Empire, and they are wanted by our enemies.

I commit the message to memory then snap open the metal cap of my lighter, sparking the wick to flame. I set the edge of the message alight, and while moving toward the door to the head, rotate the paper to spread the flame. Before the fire burns my fingers, I drop it into the toilette where it sizzles and smokes in the bowl of water. The writing is gone, crinkled into black ash.

今

I**T'S TWO DAYS TO** O**LESK.** Uneventful days for me, but not for the soldiers on the train, who seem to have no end of drink and cards. I know we near Olesk when the vodka dries up and the cards disappear. The soldiers know their party is over.

Olesk lies on the eastern edge of the Empire. The character of the town is distinctly eastern, distinctly Quin–squat, square buildings, soot-blackened, with roof eaves pulled into delicate points like they were made of taffy. Built during the past fifty years as the Empire expanded its influence toward the rising sun, Olesk grew in importance as coal veins were found in the frozen taiga and plains of Sibersk.

The station at Olesk is accustomed to dealing with freight, not people. The wide platforms are packed with flywheel lifts, steam cranes, hand barrows, shovels, ropes and the like. When my train arrives, it looks as if the equipment has been reluctantly pulled to the side to make a narrow egress for the soldiers and the handful of other passengers. They haven't bothered to sweep the black dust, and it takes to the air among the soldier boots and quickly coats the hem of my long coat with fine soot.

I check my pocketwatch. I have less than an hour to find the Karakulov Market.

The soldiers mill around on the platform, clogging the way to the stairs up. I try to pass through, begging pardon at first, but then push more forcefully when politeness falls on deaf ears. I reach the end of the platform and break free from the mass of soldiers and onto the steps leading up into the station itself.

Olesk may not handle many passengers, but the station is large and has capacity for many trains. All girders and raw stone, the construction is brutal and utilitarian, unlike the Grand Station in Aurestapol, which is a work of art by the finest craftsmen of the Empire. That Olesk's station would be devoid of people seems unlikely, yet only a man with a hook where his hand should be pushes a broom across the floor of the vast, empty lobby.

In the center of the lobby is a café surrounded by five small wrought iron tables. The small café building is closed up by metal grilles over each of the four sides. At one of the tables sits a man in a dark suit. The pinstriping elongates his already large form. His hat sits on the table next to a flask and shot glass of clear liquid–vodka most likely. He looks up from his hand resting on the table next to the glass.

I am caught in my tracks. "Krauss?"

The man shows no surprise at seeing me. He has dark hair cut neat and short, and swept to the right over his brow. His eyes look black in the dimness. A shadow of stubble blackens his jaw like coal soot. The corners of his mouth rise slightly.

It is Krauss. I've not seen him since El Emir, and

that's not a bad thing either.

Krauss is a Red Cuff and suspicious of everything. He sees insurgents in every shadow and spies in every face. In El Emir he had me thrown into a cell because he was convinced I was passing intelligence to the Papalate. When I eventually walked away, he wasn't pleased.

Krauss drains the shot glass and sets it down on the table with a clang that echoes through the station. "Calypto," he says, contempt obvious in his voice. He motions to the chair opposite him at the table.

"I'm in a hurry," I say.

"I insist." He opens his coat and flashes the handle of his FP.

As if that would scare me, yet I know he will follow me, likely even try to arrest me again if I don't give him his due. I set my bag on the floor and settle into the chair.

Krauss pours another shot of vodka into the only glass and slides it across the table to me. He tips the metal flask in my direction. "To the motherland and victory," he says.

We drink, me from the glass, he directly from the flask.

It's good vodka, but I expect nothing less from Krauss. He likes his vodka, and unlike most, he has old money to afford quality.

"How long has it been?" he asks after he's poured me another drink.

I leave the shot on the table and keep an eye on Krauss. Nothing feels … wrong here, but I know that everything about Krauss is wrong. Yet, dislike him as I do, men like Krauss are necessary, especially during tough times. That doesn't excuse what he did to me.

"El Emir, no?" He grins at me. When his eyes flick down to the glass on the table, I wave toward it with my hand. He drains the shot with a toss of his head. "I am sorry about El Emir," he says, putting the glass down. "Business, you know. No hard feelings?"

If Krauss wasn't so dangerous, I would have crossed my arms to show my displeasure, but doing so would rob me of that split second that could be the difference between life and death. Instead I keep my hands flat on my lap. Tension makes my shoulders ache, but I don't dare lower my guard for a second.

Krauss frowns at my lack of response. He then waves his hand, brushing away hurt feelings as if they were crumbs on the table. "No matter," he says.

This game of his has gone on too long. "Why are you here?" I ask.

"That is not the right question," he says. "No, no. The right question is why are *you* here?"

I say nothing. The Red Cuffs and my organization have a history of conflict. The Order has always had wide latitude in its operations, and I must admit, I've never truly understood the entire range of its activities. When R recruited me into The Order, she had simply said our purpose was to maintain the Empire. The Red Cuffs, however, are tasked with protecting the Empire. Those missions may sound the same, and certainly ours encompasses theirs, but they are, in fact, very different. We don't look for the enemy, per se. Krauss hunts the enemy, wherever it might be, whoever it might be.

"I'm on assignment," I tell him. Surely he knows this already and there is no harm in telling him as much.

"In Olesk?"

I'm almost offended the way he plays stupid with me. Of course in Olesk. Why else would I be here? It's almost as if he's goading me into saying more than is good for me.

"Yes, yes, of course," he says, a smile now splitting his face.

"I, too, am on assignment. Here in Olesk." He raises his hands as if to encompass the city. "This magnificent shit hole. I am looking for enemies of the Empire. They lurk everywhere in this place. Quin spies. Papalate sympathizers. I then hear that you are on a train–I have ears everywhere, you know–and I wonder, 'What is Calypto doing coming here, to this den of subversion?' so I come to find out. Not that I doubt your loyalty," he adds hastily.

He didn't doubt my loyalty in El Emir either. At least that's what he kept telling me even as he raised welts on my back. "If you have a question about why I'm here, send it up your chain."

"It is faster to ask you, friend to friend. You understand." He grins at me again, and it unsettles my stomach. "No? You're not going to tell me? Well, not to worry, Calypto. But some words of warning for you, friend to friend. Olesk is a dangerous place. The Empire has been too complacent, in my opinion, and allowed a dangerous element to fester too long. This city is a pus-filled boil and I'm here to lance it. Finish your business quickly, and leave. Do not cross me, or El Emir will seem like a vacation at Tanev." When he finishes speaking, he leans across the table. All semblance of a smile is gone.

I keep my face expressionless, but wonder how he knew I was on that train. The Red Cuffs are not to be underestimated, but his knowledge of my movement is disconcerting.

Krauss rises, and the swiftness of his movement draws me to my feet, crouched and ready to protect myself, but he makes no move toward me. Instead, he sweeps the shot glass into his hand and slips it into the pocket of his coat. He raises the flask toward his lips as if to drink, but stops and shakes the now empty container. He screws on the cap and slips it into his coat's other pocket. Turning, Krauss leaves me alone in the station.

今

Everything in Olesk is covered in a layer of
oily soot. The stone buildings are blackened, the
wheels of the autos and trams leave marks on the
roadway. The air is heavy with the stink of sulfur,
which burns my throat and makes my lungs ache. The
morning sun should be over the horizon, but I can't
see anything but a heavy gray haze of fog and soot.

Unlike the capital, the streets outside the station
are narrow and congested. People bustle by on foot
and three-wheeled bicycles. Women trudge under the
burden of large baskets. They wear thick gray coats
that look made from handspun cloth, something
other than wool. The shops spill across the sidewalks
and into the street with racks of woolen shirts and
coats, carts laden with spoons and lacquer bowls.
Young girls fan the soot away from fur-lined boots,
but it is a losing battle.

Soldiers with rifles and bayonets loiter on the
corners smoking hand-rolled cigarettes and leering at
the women.

I ask a shopkeeper for directions to the Karakulov

Market. He's an old man with olive skin and features part Quin. He tries to sell me a set of dice and a watch, but when he sees I'm not interested, he tells me where to go.

Karakulov Market lies in an open square near the city center. The perimeter of the market is a pavilion of covered stalls, numbered sequentially, staffed with vendors, most of them from outlying areas based on the rustic nature of their coats and the prevalence of agricultural products. The center of the square is exposed to the elements and packed with women and men on ragged blankets to mark their territory. Spread across the blankets are their wares, usually a meager array of jarred preserves, a half dozen sickly fish snared from some oily lake, chicken feet and pig knuckles, embroidered handkerchiefs, a dozen darkly lacquered hair sticks, or a single crudely sewn shirt. Most of the vendors look of Quin decent, a lingering testament of the ethnic heritage of this frontier of the Empire.

I gently remove the hand of a hawker from my sleeve and push my way through the shifting crowd. For such a pathetic market, the crowd is large. I move my bag to hang along my abdomen, where it will be a harder target for thieves. As I pass stalls in the pavilion, the haggling is in at least three different languages. In addition to the Empire's tongue, I also recognize Quin and one of the languages spoken in the Sultanate to the south. How many of these people are the insurgents that Krauss has been sent to ferret out?

No one bothers me as I move with purpose through the crowd. The mass of people generates its own warmth, and the pavilion provides shelter from the wind. Fragrant smoke drives away the sulfur stink. If the press of the unwashed crowd hadn't been so persistent, the market may have been pleasant.

As I near the rendezvous site, I check my watch. I'm early.

Birdie hasn't arrived yet, so I pass by the meeting location and continue around the pavilion again, this time stopping at the stalls and feigning interest. I watch the crowd, but if anyone is following me, I don't detect them. My stomach growls, and I buy three meat sticks—three strips of some whitish meat, chicken maybe, threaded onto wooden skewers and roasted over coals. I don't recognize the spices, but the meat is flavorful.

I time my route to arrive back at the meeting site at the appointed hour. As I near the corner of stall 734, I see a woman in a gray shawl, the back intricately embroidered with an owl, wings spread across her shoulder blades as if ready to take flight. Or maybe to land. The hood of her cloak is pulled up, hiding her face from me.

I move next to her and wait for her to acknowledge me.

She sets down the scarf she is examining, a hand-knitted red strip with a band of white birds near the fringed end. "Punctual as always, Calypto," she says without looking at me.

"Heard anything interesting lately?" I ask. Birdie has a knack for learning things. She hears things that others don't, almost as if information is drawn to her, like filings to a magnet.

"Lots," she says, but doesn't elaborate. She must sense my unease because she says, "It's safe here and I'm sure I wasn't followed."

"Neither was I."

"I would expect nothing less." She flashes a sidelong grin at me. Birdie has a slender face with a pointed chin and white-white skin, like high clouds in a winter sky. Her blond bangs obscure turquoise eyes. She is one of the few people I know in The Order, having been recruited at the same time—me from an orphanage in Kirov; she from somewhere north of the arctic circle.

"I ran into Krauss at the station this morning."

Birdie's smile collapses into something ugly. "I heard he was here, but I've had the good fortune of not running into him. Word is he's exterminating revolutionary cells. A group called the Silver Tigers locally, but officially going by the more prosaic People's Revolution. They have delusions of grandeur, but strictly small time, I hear. What better task for someone like Krauss?"

Listening to Birdie, I wonder if the small-time revolutionaries might have tried to make a big-time statement. "There was an assassination attempt in Aurestapol the morning I left—"

"Not an attempt," she says. "Someone named Alexander Olstevski."

I hadn't heard who or if it had been successful. News travels fast, at least for Birdie. "Never heard of him."

"Me neither." Birdie sounds perplexed by the admission, and I am too. It's not often Birdie hasn't heard something. Either no one knows anything about this Olstevski, or they're not talking. Either development is unusual in my experience. "But my ears are open." Her tone suggests that it's only a matter of time before she hears something.

"I saw it happen," I say, "but I didn't stick around."

"That was smart."

"Could these Tigers have done it?"

"Word is the Papalate is behind it."

"I think that's what we're supposed to believe."

"But you don't."

"I don't know what to believe," I say.

"But you don't believe the Papalate did it."

I shake my head slowly, betraying my uncertainty. "It just … feels wrong. I know everything points to the Papalate, but that's what bothers me. I can't explain it."

Birdie hums a note of what might be agreement or skepticism. "Sometimes a wart is simply a wart."

I take the envelope with the drawing of the tattoo from my coat pocket and hand it to Birdie.

"What's this?" she asks.

"I was hoping you might know."

Birdie rotates the drawing.

"It's a kanji symbol," she says. "Quin writing, but I don't know what it means. Of course I could also be entirely wrong."

"You ever see something like it before?"

Birdie shrugs. "Why do you ask?"

"The assassin had it tattooed on his neck." I fold the paper and return it to my pocket. "If you hear anything …"

"I'll let you know. But you're on another job, aren't you?" Birdie reaches under her shawl and removes a folded newspaper—the local rag, considering the smeared ink and its lack of heft. I take it from her, my brow crinkling. A newspaper? How is a newspaper a Class-A delivery?

Casually I look into the fold, finding two train tickets back to Aurestapol. When I look up, someone else has joined us. Where she came from, I don't know, but based on the simple cut of her shawl, which resembles many of those in the market, she was likely standing nearby, maybe right next to Birdie.

"This is Lera," Birdie says. "You'll see her safely back to Aurestapol."

I barely hear Birdie's words; my attention is focused on the young woman next to her. Or should I say girl? She doesn't look older than fifteen and she's tiny, even next to Birdie. From the shape of her features, she is of mixed heritage, Quin and something else I can't place. She wears a long coat and scarf piled thickly around her neck. A tightly wound knot of thick black hair is piled high onto the top of her head and held in place with a half dozen barrettes. But all of this I notice in passing because my attention is drawn immediately to the thick glasses covering her eyes. They are not so much eyeglasses as aviator goggles, held to her face by a thick strap running around the back of her head. Peering out at me through these googles are the largest eyes I have ever seen—freakishly large and milky white. She has no irises, no pupils, not even a shadow of color like in an old person's eyes that are cloudy with cataracts. Lera's eyes are simply smooth, glassy white orbs, like pearl onions.

"There must be a mistake," I say after a long pause in which the world seems to freeze motionless around me.

"What do you mean?" Birdie asks.

"I'm here for a Class-A *package*."

"You're here for a Class-A," Birdie says. I hear an

edge in her tone that says *don't question me*. "You're here to escort Lera safely to Aurestapol."

"They didn't tell me ..." How could R not have told me? Did she know? She had to have known.

Carrying a package is one thing. Being responsible for a life is something entirely different, especially when it's a Class-A, meaning deliver at all cost or destroy so it doesn't fall into enemy hands. That second part is what bothers me as I stand there. I've killed before, yes. I'll kill again, certainly. But Lera is not my enemy. She is not trying to kill me. This isn't a case of kill or be killed.

Birdie grabs my elbow, and I pull away from her.

"I can't take her."

Birdie puts her arm around my shoulder and leans in close to me so she is all I can see. She smells of freshly fallen snow.

"You've never escorted a new recruit," she says. "I understand your concern, but she's important. She needs your help, and whatever you may think, you were chosen for this mission because The Order believes you are the right person for the job."

"But how can she be a Class-A?" I know it's a stupid question as it's crossing my lips. Why can't a person be Class-A? The fact she's a living person doesn't mean she isn't important to The Order and would be dangerous if falling into the wrong hands.

"Every recruit is a Class-A," Birdie says.

A lump rises in my throat as I remember the kindly looking, gray-haired man who had escorted me from the orphanage in Kirov to Aurestapol. He had bought me fried cheesecakes with sour cream and jam on the train. Would he have done what was necessary to keep me from falling into the wrong hands?

Of course he would have. That is why we work for The Order—we do as we're instructed for the good of the Empire.

I shake my head and turn away; this is a losing battle. Birdie probably knows it too, but she gives me space to reach that conclusion on my own. I have no choice; I can tell myself I won't do it, but in the end, I will do what I must. I always do, for the good of the Empire.

I remove the tickets from the newspaper. They are for the noon train back to Aurestapol. I drop the paper on the ground and tuck the tickets into my pocket.

"What about her?" I lift my bearded chin in Lera's direction. Lera isn't paying attention, but I speak softly. A vendor is attempting to sell her a scarf, which is ridiculous considering the perfectly good one wrapped around her neck.

"An orphan." Birdie doesn't elaborate—there's no need to because it's a common story for those I know in The Order. "We're not the only ones showing an interest, either."

My eyebrow ticks up. "Papalate?"

"Don't know. The orphanage mistress, Ms. Okimoto, wasn't overly helpful. She just seemed happy someone wanted her."

"She didn't know about her talent?"

"Not in the strictest sense, no."

I murmur understanding. Like most of us, Lera probably learned at a young age to hide her talent or risk getting teased or beaten or ostracized. Children are cruel creatures to those who are different, and looking at Lera, she is very different.

"Is she blind?"

"Not really, but her vision isn't very good."

Lera holds the scarf she's inspecting close to her nose, almost as if she's sniffing the wool. I wonder how far she can see, and how much of a problem this could be. If we got separated by a few meters, would she even be able to find me?

"What is her talent?" I ask

Birdie shrugs. "She won't say, but we think it's something to do with her eyes."

"We *think*? We don't know?"

"Did they know what you could do? Really do, I mean?"

"Fair enough," I say. It became apparent early in my training that The Order didn't know the full extent of my talent when they recruited me. Only later, after I had come to trust my handler, did I explain it to them.

"We've been watching her for a few weeks, but we can't risk leaving her–"

But I'm not paying attention any longer.

One stall over, a vendor helps a woman with her blond hair pulled up under a tall fur hat remove a coat she was trying on. On the back of the woman's neck is the same tattoo as on the assassin in Aurestapol. The woman hastily pulls her own coat back on and snaps the collar up to her ears.

"What is it?" Birdie asks.

"That woman," I say, pointing with a flick of my eyes. "She has the same tattoo."

"As the assassin?"

The woman appears to have decided against the coat and bows to the vendor then turns away from the stall. Unlike nearly everyone else I've seen in Olesk, she has no Quin heritage in her. Her profile is angular, like chipped flint, and she's solidly built, tall and thick necked, but not fat. She is all lean muscle, like that on a swimmer.

"That can't be coincidence," I say. "They're linked."

The woman starts off into the crowd away from us. For now, her tall fur hat is easy to see.

"Is it safe here?" I ask.

Birdie's lips press into a thin line as she considers the situation. This is probably irresponsible on my part–I should worry about my mission–but what if this is something bigger? It would be even more irresponsible to ignore it.

Birdie must have reached the same conclusion, because she jerks her head in the direction of the woman in the hat and says, "Go."

I drop my bag at Birdie's feet and delve into the crowd.

Outside the market, the woman stops and surveys the street, giving the moments I need to catch up. At the entrance to the market, I feign interest in a pair of boots, drawing the hopeful eye of the man tending the stall. When the woman moves on, I put down the boots and follow.

She leads me through the streets of Olesk, and the gentle black sootfall. The wind off the Andrusk Sea is cold. I pull up the collar of my long coat as much for warmth as to hide my face; not that I think it would matter. I've never seen this woman before, and likely she's never seen me either. She doesn't look like a Papalate agent, but then they can take any form, right? I wonder for a moment if the dual tattoos could be coincidence. Humans crave patterns, seeing them even when they are not really there. Part of my initial training for The Order was to hone my mind to question what I think is true, to delve through the noise to find the signal. It's just as important to know when there's no signal as it is to find one.

But this has to be more than coincidence.

We pass grimy stone buildings whose architecture predates the transcontinental rail. Away from the Karakulov Market, the crowd grows sparse and shadowing her becomes more challenging. I drift back, so that I'm more than a block behind, nervous now that if she detects me and runs, she'll slip away.

She makes several turns, and once I think she looks back at me, making me paranoid now that I'm being led into a trap. Yet the world still feels right–my talent is quiet–and her head turn must have been a trick of my mind. With each left or right she makes, I find us in a narrower, darker street. The buildings have gone from stone to wood and stucco with tile roofs. Several have cross-timbers the diameter of my thighs, carved with interlocking geometric patterns that look distinctly eastern.

Finally she turns off the street, dropping down a short flight of stairs, and goes through a green door into a basement room.

I hustle down the empty street to the top of the stairs. Over the door is a sign with peeling paint that says "The Green Door Café."

I stand there for a good minute, trying to decide what to do. My moment of truth. Do I walk away, accept the official version–the assassination was carried out by the Papalate–or do I follow my instinct and go through the peeling green door? If I go down there, what am I waking into?

This isn't my mission. My mission is to bring a

half-blind girl back to Aurestapol. A half-blind girl I'm expected to kill if there's any chance she will fall into enemy hands. She has to be more important than going through that green door, no matter how much I may believe I'm right.

I start to turn back toward the Karakulov Market, but I stop after a step. There is more here. I sense it. I know it. I can't walk away without doing something.

The door isn't locked. Cigarette smoke rides the yellowish light out onto the dingy landing—pungent tobacco, cheap and sour smelling, and strong booze that reeks of impurities, likely distilled in a back room from old potatoes. A half dozen tables fill a cramped space to the right of a long bar of nicked wood. The tables are full of men playing cards or dice, while they drink and smoke hand-rolled cigarettes. Several more people line the bar, some sitting on three-legged stools while others stand in tight circles talking and drinking. No one seems to notice me except the man behind the bar, who glares as I stand in the open doorway, letting in the cold. I close the green door, and the man nods his approval while he finishes pouring a shot of cloudy liquid.

The tattooed woman sits at a table with a dozen people. She's removed her coat and laid it across her lap, but she's left on her fur hat. Five of the men play what looks to be mahjong, although I've never actually seen the game, but what else could they be playing with ivory tiles in this part of the world? They wear wool suit coats with silver cuffs. I assume the top hats hung on the rack in the corner belong to them, but that might be presumptuous; no one else in the place looks like the type to own hats like that. The rest of the place is filled with an odd assortment of men in long-sleeved linen shirts, short jackets, women in wool dresses and long skirts that scrape the tops of their black shoes.

Not wanting to drawn attention, I squeeze into an open space at the bar.

"Vodka," I say.

The bartender claps a shot glass onto the bar and half fills it. Before he can turn away, the man next to me chides him and says something in a language that sounds familiar, but which I don't understand– perhaps a local dialect. The barkeep adds a plate next to my shot glass and adorns it with several cuts of smoked fish, a few chunks of boiled potato flecked with green dill, and two slices of pickled beet. Before turning away, he refills the man's shot glass.

"Forgive Izan. He's a good man when you get to know him," the stranger at my elbow says. He tips his vodka back, drains the glass, then stabs a potato chunk with his small fork and shoves it into his mouth. He has an odd-shaped nose, as if his left nostril had been damaged as a child and grown back differently from the right. "He distills the best vodka in Olesk and his *zakuski* are good, so it's easier to overlook his shortcomings," the man continues. "His secret is his abhorrence to filtering out the flavor. Whoever thought vodka needed filtering was an idiot. You are not going to drink?"

I down my drink. Indeed the vodka is exceptional– a rich earthy flavor that is pleasant on the tongue and warm-but-not-harsh as it goes down my throat. The smoked fish practically melts in my mouth.

The stranger slaps his palm on the top of the bar and Izan refills both our glasses. At the man's insistence, Izan reluctantly leaves the bottle.

"I am Alexei," the man says, raising his glass.

I grunt noncommittally and don't look at him, hoping he'll get the message that I'm not interested in talking.

"No name, friend? That is fine. Names can be dangerous in these uncertain times."

My shot glass hesitates momentarily on its course to my lips, and I see from Alexei's grin that he notices it.

"Yes, uncertain times," he says slowly, quietly.

His tone raises the hairs on the back of my neck. The light in the bar seems to take on a brownish hue and the conversations that had filled the place become muffled, as if Alexei and I have been dragged down a long hall together away from the others.

"My name is not really Alexei, but you can call me that. Just as Mr. Calypto is not your name either. Shh. Don't look so surprised, and don't worry; your secret is safe with me."

I decide not to reach for my FP. If Alexei had wanted me dead, he would have tried so already.

"How do you know my name?" I drain my vodka and try to look unfazed even though sweat prickles my forehead and starts pooling in the small of my back. This time I chase the vodka with a pickled beet.

"Sit with me. You will be interested in what I have to say."

Taking the vodka bottle, he leaves me at the bar and goes to a table in the back corner. The group that had been at the table vacates it, and Alexei sits so his back is to the wall and faces the door. He nudges the chair next to him toward me in invitation.

I take my glass and the plate of *zakuski* and join Alexei, sitting in the other chair that also puts my back to the wall, instead of the one he offered me.

Alexei grins at me. One of his front teeth is chipped. "One can never be too cautious," he says.

From where I sit, I can see the tattoo on the neck of the woman who led me here.

"It means 'now,'" Alexei says, nodding in the direction of my gaze.

"Now?"

"Yes. As in the present. Today. You know, live in the today, live in the now." Alexei finishes the last piece of smoked fish. He refills our glasses. "You have seen that mark before."

"What do you know about that mark?"

"Do you know who you work for?" Alexei asks.

"Is this a trick question?"

"You think you know, but you don't." Alexei jabs his glass toward me to punctuate his comment. He empties it and refills it again from the almost empty bottle. His cheeks are pink, but he still sounds a long way from drunk.

I, on the other hand, need to slow down.

"What does that mean?"

"You get your orders, yes? But do you know where they come from? Do you really know where they come from?"

The edges of my mouth pull down into a frown. What is he getting at? Does he know who I work for? He knows who I am, so is it unrealistic to assume he knows about The Order too? That would make him–I'm not sure what that makes him.

"You see now, yes?" Alexei continues smugly. "But you think: it's for the good of the Empire."

"I know it's so," I say without hesitation.

"How can you be sure?"

I finish my vodka and chase it with the last chunk of potato. My stomach feels hollow and the vodka burns it. "Who is she? Silver Tigers?"

Alexei shrugs.

"They are insurgents?"

Alexei shrugs again. His coyness begins to annoy me. I'm wasting time here, when I should be escorting Lera back to Aurestapol. Does it matter if some radical insurgent group or a Papalate assassin killed some low dignitary? The end result is ultimately the same.

"Who do you work for?"

"There are many things you need to learn on your own in order to truly believe them," Alexei says.

As he's speaking, a shiver rips down my spine. The noise in the room stops for a moment, as if a reel-to-reel has come untracked. My vision stutters and the world slides forward again at break-neck speed. I duck a fraction of a second before the door splinters open, hitting the floor on my hands and knees behind the table. It takes another moment for the first screams to sound, but by then I know it's too late. Glasses break. Chairs tumble over as people flee for cover. Alexei tumbles face down on the floor next to me. On his shirt, small red circles are expanding–fletchette holes drilled clear through his heart and body.

I scurry across the floor toward the bar. A woman tumbles over my back, but I don't slow. Over two fallen men, one still alive but making a gurgling noise as he bleeds into his lungs. He will be dead in less than a minute as blood puddles under him from the hole in his neck. Flechettes thunk into the wooden wall. Bottles behind the bar shatter. I am amazed people are still moving, but then realize it hasn't been more than a second. Time stretches in such instances; the screams draw out, the splinters of wood tumble as if falling through oil.

I reach the space behind the bar. Izan stares at me with glassy lifeless eyes and a growing red button on his forehead. I draw my FP. I have been in a gunfight before, but my hand shakes uncontrollably; my mind is a blur of white noise. Without conscious thought, I pressurize the weapon and remove the safety. Training is the key, the weapon master who instructed me always preached. It's impossible to think clearly in a gunfight, so training is the difference between life and death. I don't know why I think this—maybe as a way to calm myself, and it seems to work. My hand is steady now.

A dozen flechettes ping off the shattered mirror behind the bar and bounce around my boots, leaving thin red lines on the floor. The flechettes are rifle caliber, and from the rate of fire, there are at least three rifles and also the higher-pitched sound of several pistols. I'm severely outgunned, and whoever they are, they seem intent on killing everyone.

Movement catches my eye, and I swing my pistol around. In the corner under the bar where it meets the wall, a hand extends from a dark opening and motions me to follow. The screaming has stopped; the only sound now is the discharge of the weapons. I crawl over the top of the dead bartender and through the darkened opening into a narrow space.

The woman with the tattoo raises her finger to her lips then reaches across me in the cramped space to slide the panel back into place.

A hidden space inside the bar, probably to hide

contraband or fugitives. Just enough light filters through a small vent that looks out into the café for me to see the woman's wide eyes, her disheveled hair. She's lost her fur hat and struggles to keep her breathing quiet in the suddenly silent café.

"Count them up," says one of the attackers. I recognize the voice immediately; there's no mistaking it. Krauss.

Boots scuffle along the plank floor as they drag and stack bodies. A shadow passes in front of the vent. The woman bites the knuckles of her right hand.

Within a few seconds, it's hot enough in the hiding place to coax sweat from me.

"He's not here, captain, but this one's alive," says one of Krauss's men.

A woman yelps, presumably as one of Krauss's men drags her across the floor to him.

"I'm looking for Valentin," Krauss says. "Where is he?"

The woman says something, but it's unintelligible through her sobs.

"You know who I'm talking about," Krauss says. "Tell me."

More sobs. Someone slaps her, likely Krauss, and the woman starts wailing.

"Shut up," Krauss says, but the woman continues to cry. "Get her out of here." Her screams fade as Krauss's men drag her out of the café.

The woman next to me bites harder into her knuckles.

"No one in the back," says another of Krauss's men. "Maybe the tip was wrong and he wasn't here."

Krauss swears and knocks over a chair. "Let's go."

"And them?"

"Insurgent scum. Leave them as a warning."

Once the footsteps have left, the woman releases her knuckle and wipes her eyes. "We need to leave," she says, surprising me with her sudden level-headedness. A moment ago she looked about scream. Now she's steady and businesslike.

"Thank you," I say as she reaches across me and slides open the panel. I wriggle out feet first and she follows me. I stop her from standing up, and I keep my FP out as we crouch behind the bar. I wouldn't put it past Krauss to leave someone behind, just in case.

I peek over the top of the bar and quickly duck back down. A shadow obscures the light coming in through the crack along the bottom of the green door.

"We can get out this way." The woman crawls through a curtained doorway at the other end of the bar.

I make sure the guard hasn't moved before following the tattooed woman. On the floor near the curtain is a woman's coat, fallen from the back of a knocked over chair. I carefully collect it and slip through the curtain. She waits for me at the base of a flight of stairs that rise up to ground level. At the end of a short corridor is a battered door.

I grab her arm as she starts up the stairs. "You might want this," I say, pushing the coat into her arms. She looks at it blank-faced, but takes it. Did she know the coat's owner? "Where does that go?" I nod toward the door.

"An alley."

"He'll be watching it," I say. I don't know for

certain, but Krauss is nothing if not thorough.

"There's no other way."

"There's always another way." I squeeze past her and go to the landing at the top of the stairs. The sliver of light under the door provides barely enough illumination to see. I run my fingers along the wall, feeling for a break in the wallpaper but don't find one. I creep back down the stairs and search the wall at the bottom. As I work, I ask, "What's your name?"

"You can call me Dai Li."

"That's a name?"

"My father was Quin."

I look at her skeptically, but in the darkness I doubt she sees my expression. My fingers tick over an imperfection in the paper—a tight but discernable crack. I trace it down the wall to the wainscoting and find a narrow cut in the top of the edging. I push on the wall in several places until I eventually hear a soft click and the panel swings away from me, releasing a cool, musty smell.

Dai Li makes a soft, surprised sound.

"Where does this go?" I ask.

"How should I know?"

The rise in her tone suggests she is genuinely surprised to see the hidden door. She's likely telling the truth, which means she's not in the know on everything about this place and the people in it. "Let's go."

"But it's dark in there."

"Would you rather get shot?"

"You make a compelling argument," she says. "Lead the way."

We step into the narrow crevice, and I carefully pull the door closed until it clicks, casting us into complete darkness. I fumble a pack of matches from my pocket and scrape one across the cover, sparking it to life. The flame flares and settles down, casting a small halo on the walls of a narrow tunnel. To my left is a small shelf with a candle stub on it. I touch the flame to the wick and shake out the match before it can burn my fingers.

The wooden walls of the tunnel are barely shoulder-wide and run roughly eastward, parallel to the street and the alleyway and under the row house that holds the café–probably a smuggling tunnel, and from the presence of the candle stub, likely still active. It must lead somewhere useful.

"Come on." I lead the way down the tunnel, the candle pushing the darkness in front of me, Dai Li's shoes clicking behind me. The walls brush against the shoulders of my long coat. I know it's my imagination, but it feels like the walls are closing in on me, like a slowly turned vise. My shirt is damp with sweat.

After thirty or forty meters, we come to the end of the tunnel, and I sigh with relief. I stand the candle stub on another small shelf and slide my hands over the smooth wooden wall until I find the release. The door opens into a dim cellar, lit by a single dingy window high on the wall. The air is damp and musty, smelling of mildew and rotting wood. A crude flight of stairs rises up to a door.

Hearing nothing through the door, I crack it. The hallway beyond is dark; a closed door is to my left. At the end of the short corridor another door leads out to the alley.

Dai Li pushes past me and peers cautiously out the curtain covering the door's small window. "It looks clear," she says, pulling on the coat. "Look like you belong." She opens the door and steps out into the alley. She turns away from the café and sets a brisk pace.

I hustle to catch up with her then grab her right arm and loop it through my left, leaving my pistol hand free. She is slightly taller than me, and says nothing of my maneuver, but tightens her hold, pulling us shoulder to shoulder.

"Who are you?" I ask.

"I've told you."

"That's not what I mean. The mark on your neck. The café."

We turn up a narrow alley between two buildings and step out onto the street. Two of Krauss's men stand guard in front of the Green Door Café. Dai Li turns us away from them, an easy gait to her walk. She is no normal woman. She hasn't questioned anything that has happened, as if having two dozen people killed around her is an everyday occurrence.

Either she knows what that was all about, or she doesn't think I can enlighten her. One of those assumptions is true, and I suspect both of them are.

"Alexei said you're part of the Silver Tigers," I say.

She falters for a step but regains her stride. "Alexei never did know when to shut up."

She won't have to worry about that anymore. From the slight crack in her voice, I realize she knows that. Then the blemish on her veneer is gone, and a hardness comes back to her voice, her features. "He also didn't know as much as he thought he did."

"So you are with the Silver Tigers?"

"It's complicated," she says, "and you're not ready for me to explain it." There's a finality to her tone that tells me she won't say any more about it.

"Some things I need to learn on my own to really believe them," I say.

She flashes a weak smile.

"Maybe you don't give Alexei enough credit." The jab feels good for a moment, only to have that brief victory chased away with a pang of guilt at the cheap shot. "Why did you help me?"

"Maybe someone up there likes you. Or at least they still need you." Her look, stony and compassionless, pauses me in my tracks. She walks another stride before our looped arms stop her. Flecks of black soot freckle her nose. "You don't realize the danger you're in. Get out of Olesk while you still can. Next time I might not be able to help you." She slips her arm free from mine with such ease it could have been greased. Spinning sharply on her heels, she continues on her way, her hips swaying like a pendulum.

I sense I'll learn nothing more from her, so I watch as she vanishes into the crowd before turning back toward the Karakulov Market.

今

AS I APPROACH, Birdie looks up nervously from her watch and exhales a sigh of relief. "What took you so long?"

Lera huddles close to her side, clutching a small shoulder bag with a long strap slung across her chest. She doesn't look particularly concerned, but then I can't really read her expression because of her milky eyes.

"I narrowly avoided a run-in with Krauss," I say.

"And?"

I shrug. "Wasn't much to learn, but I think my hunch about the Silver Tigers was right."

"They pulled the trigger in Aurestapol?" She sounds surprised, and with good reason.

Why assassinate an unknown government official if you're attempting to overthrow the Empire. If you want to make a statement, at least shoot someone people have heard of. Unless there's something more to know about our dead man, this Alexander Olstevski.

Birdie hands me my bag. "You better get moving.

You don't want to spend any longer in Olesk than necessary."

"I know; it's not safe."

Birdie cocks her head quizzically at me.

"Just something I heard," I say.

"Take care of her, Calypto," Birdie says.

We shake hands and Birdie leaves me alone in the market with Lera, who stares at me with those huge white eyes. They blink slowly, not frequently enough to be what I would consider normal, but nothing about them is normal. The way she stares at me makes my scalp tingle.

"You ready to go?" I ask, not really expecting an answer.

"I'm not blind," she says.

"I didn't think you were."

"You wouldn't be the first to think that."

"I imagine not."

"I'm sixteen. I don't need a nanny."

"I'm not your nanny," I say, a little more edge in my voice than I expected. "I'm your escort."

"Why couldn't Birdie escort me?"

"Because that's my job." When she starts to say something else, I cut her off. "We can discuss this once we catch our train, okay?"

Lera makes a little snorting sound but doesn't say anything else.

We make our way out of the Karakulov Market and take a circuitous route through the grimy narrow streets to make sure no one is tailing us. Once I'm convinced we're not being followed, we head to the station.

PART II

INTO THE SNOW

今

THE SOLDIERS HAVE MOVED OUT, and the station is sparsely filled with civilians wearing gray jackets that were in style a decade ago, and long skirts in muted tones. The click of shoes and murmured conversations echo in the vaulted lobby. At the far end of the station, the schedule board is barely visible through the sooty air.

Lera sticks by my side, her large eyes fixed forward. Can she even see the schedule board? Or the stairs down to the platform? All the way back to the station, she stayed at my side, maybe a step behind so she could respond to my moves. Now, in the station, she's tucked herself in on my hip, just behind my arm. With every step, she presses against my side. The sensation is claustrophobic–she's invading my personal space–but I'd rather her too close than lost in the crowd.

I check the ticket: an eleven o'clock departure. The schedule board says the train is on time at platform seven; my pocket watch tells me we have fifteen minutes.

At the stairs down to our train, I'm suddenly tossed by a wave of vertigo severe enough that I grab the railing to stop from falling.

Lera stumbles to a stop at the top of the stairs and looks at me, frowning.

A shiver ripples down my spine as the world stutters forward again.

The stairwell is dark, except for the bottom, where watery light filters in from the platform. Two long shadows slide across the light on the floor. Whoever they are, they're waiting for us. Of that, I am certain.

"Change of plans," I say, and turn back into the main concourse.

"What do you mean?" Lera asks, hustling to stay close to me.

I don't want to scare her, but I also don't want to lie to her. Is she aware that others might also be interested in her and what that might mean? Probably not.

Lera's brow pinches into a crease of confusion. It's not a look of concern or fear, although it probably should be.

"I'll explain later," I say, hoping to short circuit a discussion best left for later.

At the window, I slide the tickets through the slot and under the glass. "I'd like to change these for a different train."

"The next direct is the day after tomorrow," the agent says.

I stifle a curse. "Do you have anything else leaving today?"

"I have a thirteen-ten through St. Stephensburg."

I nod. He takes my tickets and exchanges them with new ones. "Platform five," he says, already looking past me to the next person in line.

"Why are we changing trains?" Lera asks as we leave the counter. "This one will take longer to get there."

We edge around the stairs down to platform seven like they're a red-hot stove. The two shadows are still there, but in a few minutes, the train will leave, and they will know we're not on it. Then they will start to look for us elsewhere. We need to get out of the lobby.

"Slow down." Lera is nearly running to stay on my hip.

"It's not much farther, then we can walk."

The schedule board clacks as changing information cascades across it. The status of the Aurestapol train changes from "On Time" to "Departed."

We reach the stairs to platform five. They're empty; the train doesn't leave for several more hours.

"Come on." I grab her elbow as I look back toward platform seven.

Lera squirms in my grip. "You're hurting me."

"Then get moving."

She falls quiet and hurries down the stairs with me.

The train is already here, being watered and loaded with coal. A few passengers mill around the platform smoking cigarettes, bundled against the chill, while porters load suitcases. We board a carriage in the middle and find our compartment.

I pull the window shade so no one can see in from the platform. I do the same for the curtain on the door. The compartment is small–two benches that double as beds with luggage hammocks over top, where I stow our bags. Lera sits stiffly on the opposite bench, her face pinched and arms crossed. She hasn't made a sound since the top of the stairs.

"Why don't you take your jacket off?" I hang my long coat on the hook next to the door and straightened my suit coat to hide the lump of my FP in its shoulder holster. Lera keeps her jacket on, buttoned to her chin.

I sit on the bench opposite her.

Lera's gaze locks onto me. Her frown is a tangible menace that fills the compartment.

"I'm sorry I hurt your arm," I say, "but we needed to get out of the lobby."

She still doesn't say anything, and her adolescent truculence is starting to bother me. We need ground rules if this is going to work.

"You need to do what I say, when I say. It's for your safety."

"Safety? From what?"

"Haven't they told you anything?"

She shrugs. "Ms. Okimoto says she found a job for me. Serving the Empire, she put it. She didn't explain, but I suspect I won't be sewing uniforms."

"No." I try to remember what they told me when they took me away from the orphanage. It's been so long, I can't recall, but that alone suggests it wasn't much. If they had told me someone was potentially trying to kill me, I would have remembered that. Then again, maybe no one was.

"Anyone can sew uniforms," I say. "I suspect you can do things no one else can."

"I'm not special."

"Someone thinks you are."

"They'd be wrong." She turns sideways on the bench and pulls her knees up to her chest.

We sit like that, together but alone, for what seems like a long time, but I guess it's only a few minutes in reality. Silence has a way of distorting time, stretching it like caramel.

"You never answered my question," she says.

No, I didn't, and I don't particularly want to, but then she deserves to know the truth–at least what I know of the truth. "There are … other enemies of the Empire who may be looking for us."

"Enemies? You mean the Papalate?"

"I don't know. Therein is the problem."

"There could be others?" She considers this quietly.

I want to say something, but what is there to say? I distract myself by peering behind the shade. Nothing has changed on the platform.

"You're here to protect me?" she asks.

"I am."

"I don't need protecting, you know."

"I know," I say, sensing this is the right path. "But I have experience in things like this. Experience can't hurt."

She nods at me, and I take that as agreement that she'll do as I say. That eases some of my tension.

"What's your name?" The edge has disappeared from her voice.

"I'm called Calypto."

"What kind of name is that? Are you a superhero or something?"

I frown. I'm no superhero; if anything, I'm whatever is the opposite of a superhero. "Calypto's my field name," I explain. "Like Birdie isn't Birdie's name." When entering The Order, every recruit is given a field name and encouraged to leave their old name behind. It's a symbolic way to show we are no longer those people, but are now part of The Order.

"What's your real name?"

It's been a long time since I've heard my given name. I'm not sure I'd respond to it if someone yelled it on the street. Good riddance. Yet ... "Calypto is my real name," I say.

Lera must have realized not to pursue it anymore. She turns her face anywhere but in my direction, which is just as well.

"Will I get a field name?"

"Yes."

"So I'll do what you do then?"

"Not necessarily. It depends on where your talents lie and what's needed."

"Oh." She seems dissatisfied with that answer. "I hope I get a good name. Not something stupid. Will I get to pick it?"

"No. Unfortunately."

今

WE SPEAK A LITTLE as we wait for the train to depart, inconsequential small talk, like one would expect from two strangers on a train who anticipate knowing each other for only a few hours. The platform gradually fills with people, the carriage corridor gets loud as passengers board, banging their luggage against the walls and frames. I've marked our compartment as full, so no one bothers us, except the carriage porter, who checks our tickets and frowns skeptically at me.

"My daughter," I explain. I can't tell if he sees through the lie, but he punches our tickets and hands them back to me.

Gradually the platform empties. At thirteen-ten, the train whistle screams and the carriage rocks forward. We slide into the train tunnel and, for a few seconds, we are pitched into ink–dark, utter, complete–with only the clacking of the wheels on the track and groan of the cars as their couplings slide against each other. We come out into the gray light of the afternoon in a field of tracks running off in every direction, like a child's scribble. Gray buildings, lonely and dingy, close in on our line as we rattle northwest, across quiet streets.

An hour later we are out of the city, chugging across empty fields.

Lera is curled up in the corner of her bench staring out the window, but her eyes don't move to track any of the sparse features that occasionally break the monotony. I wonder for a moment if she's asleep or lost in thought or simply bored.

My stomach growls. The only thing I've eaten since last night were the *zakuski* with the vodka at the Green Door Café. My stomach grumbles louder, partially at its emptiness, but also at the unpleasant memory of what happened there.

"Are you hungry?"

"No," Lera says sullenly.

"Stay here and lock the door," I say, rising from the bench. She'll be safer here than walking around the train where the wrong eyes might see her. "Only open it for me." I pull the sliding door closed behind me and wait until I hear the latch clunk into place.

I head toward the back of the train. The corridor is busy with people still getting settled. Several compartment doors are open, revealing men in middle class coats and women in long dresses and jackets. At the end of the car, three children have the window open and one of them hangs out it. When he comes back in, his teeth chatter from the cold and soot covers his face and the collar of his linen shirt.

I pull the end door open and pass between the carriages. Two cars back is the dining carriage. There I get a plate of smoked fish and sweetened fried cheesecakes with sour cream and jam. The smell brings water to my mouth. I get enough for two and have it wrapped to take away.

As I head back, I am surprised between two carriages by Krauss coming the other direction. At first he does not recognize me, his forehead is crinkled and he appears lost in concentration, but there is no way for me to get out of his path. When he looks up, his eyes widen with recognition then narrow.

"What are you doing here?" he demands.

Sooty smoke whips by. It's cold between the cars, and I don't have my coat.

"Are you following me, Krauss?" I ask, avoiding his question. Based on his expression a moment ago, I know he didn't expect to find me here; therefore I'm not his target and this meeting was simply chance. I hate to attribute things to coincidence, but sometimes that is the reality.

"You're heading back to Aurestapol," he says. It's plainly not a question. "Your business in Olesk is finished already?"

I don't say anything. Obviously he is ignorant of my presence at the Green Door Café.

"Cat got your tongue? But then, you don't like to say anything without encouragement." He grins a sinister grin at me, the same one he had used in El Emir.

"You're a bastard, Krauss. You know that?"

"I get results."

I want to say "like at Green Door Café," but I'm not that stupid. "Your masters send for you?"

Krauss's grin slides off his face and his gaze flicks down to the bundle in my hands then back up to my face. It's such a quick glance I wouldn't have noticed

it if I hadn't been staring at him. The paper-wrapped
food is obviously for more than one. Drawing the
packages behind my back now will only attract more
attention and put my hands in a worse place when I
need to defend myself.

Krauss's mouth opens then closes, as if he's about
say something but changes his mind. He steps to the
side, as much to the side as the narrow space permits.
I don't want to walk past him and risk exposing my
back, so I turn to the side to make more room.

"After you," I say.

Krauss shows his, teeth—a semblance of a
predatory smile that makes my intestines squirm. "We
have to stop meeting this way," he says as he slowly
moves by me, rotating as he passes so as not turn his
back to me. "I might begin to think you're up to
something." He backs into the carriage vestibule and
slams the door closed.

What's Krauss doing on this train? Only a few
hours ago he shot up the Green Door Café, but from
what I had heard, he didn't find who he was looking
for, someone named Valentin. Krauss is a
sledgehammer, but what he did in the Green Door
Café is extreme, even for the Red Cuffs.

I check to make sure Krauss hasn't doubled back
before heading forward to my compartment. I
wonder if Valentin could be on the train, but dismiss
that idea. If he were, Krauss would have torn it apart
with his men, removing every seat, every panel, every
toilet until he found him. So why is he here then?

I slow as I near the compartment and look over
my shoulder. No one is behind me. I knuckle the
door and whisper for Lera to open it. She lets me in. I
hastily slide the door shut and fix the latch.

"I got you something to eat," I say. "It's a long trip."

She ignores me, but extends her hand and takes the paper bundle from me. She inspects the contents, but gives no indication if she finds the food satisfactory. Before I can get annoyed at her behavior, she shoves two of the cheesecakes into her mouth, barely chewing them before swallowing. She chases them with slivers of smoked fish and another cheesecake.

Maybe I should have bought more.

"Slow down," I say. "You'll make yourself sick."

The cheesecakes are exceptional. The smoked fish, likely bream, is too mild for my taste but has decent texture.

Lera doesn't seem to notice, however. She finishes all her food before I've eaten two of my cheesecakes. I offer her the remaining two and she takes them with a sheepish thank you.

Feeling I've accrued enough good will, I decide to ask, "How long have your eyes been like that?"

She blinks at me as if I've asked something inappropriate—which in proper company, I have—as if she's waiting for me to take it back. When I don't, she says, "I was born this way, the best I know."

"Yet you can see. Those glasses. They're …" I decide to tread lightly here. I've never seen glasses like those before. They seal against her face like goggles and are held tightly in place by a rubber strap around the back of her head. Through those lenses, her eyes are huge. Maybe it's a trick of magnification, but I shift uncomfortably under her white-eyed stare.

The lenses are bottle thick, yet something about them is odd. As I look at them more closely, I notice the lenses *aren't* really thick; instead–

"Is that water inside there?" I ask.

She touches her goggles lightly and lowers her face.

"I don't mean to pry–"

"Just making polite conversation, right?" From her tone, it's clear she feels my conversation is anything but polite.

"I need to know if I'm going to escort you safely to Aurestapol."

After a moment considering my justification, she answers. "Water is the only lens that works for me. Without it, I'm blind."

So she sees through water. If this is her talent, I've seen odder ones.

My lack of comment about her revelation seems to set her at ease. I've passed no judgment one way or the other, which is likely something that has never happened to her before. Talents that would interest The Order are rare, and those of us who possess them are usually branded as freaks.

"And with the goggles?" I ask.

She shrugs. "I see how I see. Mostly blurry shapes, except when things are close."

"What have the doctors said?" I ask.

"Nothing."

Her response raises my left eyebrow. I wonder if she can see that level of detail from across the compartment. I can't tell because her expression doesn't change. "Doctors aren't very smart sometimes," I say.

"Not many people are."

今

L ERA DOESN'T WANT TO TALK ANYMORE, so there is nothing much to do to pass the hours. She stretches out on the couch and dozes off, but it's too early for me to fall asleep and my nerves are too on end, especially knowing Krauss is only a few cars away. I envy Lera's naivety, even if I know it won't last much longer.

I stare out the window and listen to Lera's breathing, barely audible above the clacking of the train wheels.

We pass through fields slumbering under gray winter skies. They are somber squares of dirt and brown grass that are dozens of shades of brown and black and ochre. Quiet farmhouses, small towns, like squashed bugs on an auto windshield, slide by in the distance, bypassed by the rail line and prosperity. But these are the places that make the Empire. These are the people on whose backs the Empire eats and thrives. Some might say that the war is not here, so they have no complaint, but the war is everywhere, even if the trenches aren't dug across these fields.

Between the farmlands, forests stretch to the horizon, unbroken except for the occasional scar where the timber has been harvested. Thick with conical evergreens, they are less somber, even if their color is deep and saturated. A pack of wolves moves just inside the trees along the train corridor. They are intent on their prey and don't even notice us passing.

For someone in my position, I have seen surprisingly little of the Empire. I've probably seen more of the world beyond our borders than within them. I never had the luxury of wealth or freedom as a child. Now, when neither is such a problem, I lack the luxury of circumstance.

Slowly the darkness settles in.

I leave the lights in the compartment out, but a faint glow burns through the curtains over the compartment door's window. The world outside disappears, as if I'm looking down into a dark well. The cloud pack is thick enough to hide the moon, and a rime of ice edges the window, sparkling occasionally in the light when it flickers because of people passing in the corridor.

I cover Lera with a light blanket from a cupboard above the door. Her shoulders barely rise and fall under her gentle breathing.

The quiet moment is nice, and wrapped in the other light blanket, I feel warm and drowsy. Eventually I drift off to sleep.

今

I DREAM OF BEING BACK at the orphanage,
surrounded by the other kids, all of them bigger and
more menacing than I truly remember. The circle is
too tight for me to squeeze through. They shout
taunts at me, calling me freak because I told them I
could see the future. I can barely stand as my back
crawls with icy warning, but there's no escape. The
fists come then, and every time I try to crawl away,
they drag me back into the scrum by my ankles and
land more blows to my kidneys, my ribs.

Mrs. Markov watches from nearby, but she doesn't
stop them. "Why didn't you see this coming?" she
asks.

I taste my own blood as a boot knocks out three
of my teeth. The vision in my right eye blurs after
someone punches me in it.

I plead for Ms. Markov to help me, but she turns her
back on me. "Fortune helps those who help
themselves," she says. She leaves me to the boys
whose teeth have grown into long fangs, like those of
wolves.

LATE THE NEXT AFTERNOON, the train pulls into the station at St. Stephensburg, an industrial town in the foothills of the Central Range. To my surprise the platform is empty except for a contingent of soldiers in their browns with rifles unslung and in hand.

"What's happening?" Lera asks. She had been playing string games with a loop of yarn.

"I don't know," I say. As I rise, a commotion breaks out in the corridor, followed swiftly by a rapping on the compartment door. Instinctively, I loosen my suit coat, making it easier to reach my FP. "Move over there." I point to the corner not visible from the compartment door, and Lera obeys without question.

The rapping sounds a second time, and a voice with it. "Open up in the name of the emperor."

Through the parted curtain, I see a soldier with his hand resting on his holstered pistol. I crack the compartment door.

The corridor is loud with voices and the banging of luggage being moved.

"You will collect your luggage and detrain," the soldier says. He's young, probably his first assignment out of training. His baby face doesn't look like it's ever been shaved. In his winter browns, he's sweating in the warmth of the carriage, although with the exterior door open, the temperature is quickly dropping.

"Is this an inspection?"

"No. This train is being taken from public service. On behalf of the emperor's army, I apologize for the inconvenience, but you will be off this train in five minutes."

I know there will be no arguing with him. He is only carrying out the orders given to him, and he will not listen to any exceptions.

"Where's your commanding officer?" I ask.

"Major Chenov is on the platform. Take your belongings with you."

I try to pull the door shut, but the young soldier blocks it with his boot. He glares at me, his friendly soldier expression replaced with the stony face of a man realizing he has a potential problem on his hands. Without thinking, my hand begins to reach for my FP, but I catch myself and button my coat closed instead. I won't need the weapon here. "I'm going," I say, hoping that will be enough to get him to move on, but it doesn't.

I sling my bag over my shoulder and hand Lera hers. "Stay close," I say.

She stays on my heels as I push my way through the crowded corridor. Near the exit, a man with a gray beard and monocle, wearing an expensive suit, argues with an exasperated soldier. Two woman struggle with a trunk on the stairs to the platform until a soldier comes to assist them.

"Major Chenov?" I ask the soldier.

He points me toward the front of the train where the major stands in conversation with a circle of officers. I'm cut off by a pair of soldiers whose job appears to be intercepting civilians.

"The exit is that way." The solider points toward the platform stairs where the mass of people from the train are making their way up the tunnel.

"I just need a moment–"

"The major doesn't have a moment, sir."

I remove the worn billfold with my fake credentials and hold it up for the soldier to see. "I need to speak with the major." I start to edge around him, but he cuts me off again.

"This is a military operation. All civilians need to clear the platform."

I want to tell this soldier that I'm on an important mission for the Empire, that I need to be on that train, and that the train needs to continue on to Aurestapol, but I also know, like a good soldier, he will not budge from the orders given him.

I hold my position and look over the soldier's shoulder, hoping to catch the major's eye. If I can just catch his attention … As I watch, his circle of officers shifts, probably moving to stay warm in the cold air, and I see the man to whom the major is talking.

Krauss.

I should have known he'd be involved in this.

The soldiers are trying to push me away now, and if I resist much longer, they will get rough with me. Krauss is no friend, and I doubt he would willingly help, but he knows my face, and I may be able to use that to get the major's attention. What have I got to lose at this point?

"Krauss," I say.

The officers around Major Chenov continue to shift in the cold. Krauss has disappeared from my sight again.

"Krauss," I say, louder. The noise makes the soldiers who are trying to herd me toward the exit pause.

The major looks in my direction. The officers part and Krauss searches for who called him. When he sees me, he turns away and resumes talking to the major.

I am pushed more forcefully to the platform stairs then left there. The soldiers do not return to their post, however, but block me from the platform.

Lera stands at my side. She has pulled the hood of her cloak over her head and is looking downward, hiding her face from prying eyes.

I straighten my long coat.

The cold air nips at my nose and cheeks. The platform is emptying quickly of civilians, leaving only a contingent of soldiers.

"Let's see about another ticket," I say to Lera.

We go upstairs to the station's small and cold lobby. The place is dingy and old—yellowed paint on the claustrophobic walls, a scuffed concrete floor that looks like it once had tiles or wood on it, long since chiseled off. It is almost like the place is being renovated, but the work has been suspended due to a lack of funds. Even though it isn't even sixteen o'clock, the lobby is dark and stuffed with shadows.

A crowd presses up against the ticket window, like a kicked-up ant's nest. I learn quickly that there are no other trains today, and the next one to Aurestapol

won't arrive until the day after tomorrow.
Fortunately, they are exchanging tickets for any who
want them.

Two days in St. Stephensburg. Unacceptable.

I check my wallet. We're still a long ways from
Aurestapol, and I doubt have enough to hire an auto
that could get us there.

"What are we going to do?" Lera grips the collar of
her cloak tightly to keep out the cold.

It is an icebox inside the station. How can it be
this cold?

The ticket agent is handing out new tickets to the
grumbling crowd. If the crowd didn't have the
soldiers to take the blame, I think they would have
beaten the young man in their displeasure. As it is,
they grudgingly take the new tickets he's offering
them before leaving.

"I don't know yet," I say, watching as the crowd
thins. Our immediate need is a safe place to stay.
Then I need to contact R and see if she can help.

Back at the stairs to the platform, a half dozen
soldiers stand guard, making sure no one goes down.
"Stay close," I say, "but stay behind me."

I approach the soldiers, trying to look casual. They
stiffen as I near and inform me the platform is closed.

I light three cigarettes and offer them to the men.
They take them, and seem to relax. I am one man to
their six, and they aren't threatened by me.

"Any of you from this town?" I ask.

"Aya," says one of the soldiers around a cigarette.
"Julian." He nods toward one of the soldiers hissing
smoke from his nose. Julian nods at me, confirming
what his friend has said.

I edge closer to Julian, but also closer to the stairs,

and can now see down to the platform.

"Looks like I'll be staying the night. Can you recommend a comfortable place to stay?"

Down on the platform, a line of men in shackles shuffles toward the train. A prisoner transfer? I am not aware of any Empire prison in St. Stephensburg. And why commandeer a passenger train to transport them? Are they that dangerous?

The prisoners are hooded, so I cannot guess their nationality. So far behind the lines, St. Stephensburg is an odd place to keep prisoners of war, so maybe they are not foreigners, and instead local insurgents. St. Stephensburg is an important smelting and weapon production city, so it could attract the attention of Papalate saboteurs or internal terrorists. Perhaps the Silver Tigers?

"You want the Imperial Hotel." Julian passes the cigarette to another soldier. "If Carla is at the desk, tell her Julian sent you, and she'll take good care of you." He grins at me, and I wonder if Carla is his girl or his sister. He gives me directions to the hotel, and I thank him.

Lera and I exchange our tickets with the agent. By the time we finish, the last of the passengers are gone, and the station feels hollow, like a catacomb.

As we turn from the agent, Krauss is leaning against the wall, watching me with a pinched expression.

"Why didn't you tell me?" I ask.

"You didn't ask," he says snidely.

"We're on the same side, you know."

"According to you." He looks around me at Lera. "Why didn't you tell me you weren't alone?"

"*You* didn't ask."

Krauss grunts noncommittally. His arms are folded across his chest, but I still keep my distance. My right arm tenses, ready to reach for my weapon if Krauss makes any indication of a move. He shifts his weight, but doesn't make a motion toward me.

"Who's your friend?"

"Who are the prisoners? I thought you shot tigers, not put them in cages?" A stupid thing to say, but it wipes the grin off Krauss's face.

I don't expect to get anything more out of him, and I'm tired of looking at his smug face. I motion Lera toward the station exit, and I keep myself between her and Krauss.

"Enjoy your stay," Krauss says with a laugh.

今

SNOW FLUTTERS DOWN, pregnant flakes that already are collecting in the streets and on the tree-lined sidewalks. The snowfall is heavy enough to obscure vision in the gloom from the rapidly descending night and dense cloud pack.

The street is eerily quiet. I would expect it to be crowded with people heading home. A few autos are parked along the side of the road, but nothing moves. The buildings are dark, as if no one lives here. Even the people from the train are gone.

Snow has already collected on Lera's shoulders and the hood of her cloak. "I want to go back inside," she says.

"The hotel is nearby."

"I don't like the snow."

I grab her arm as she turns to go back into the station. The lights have gone out inside. "It's only snow," I say. Her wrist trembles in my grip. "It's not far to the hotel. Five minutes; no more. We'll be safe there." They should also have a phone I can use to reach R and find out what assistance is nearby.

I gently pull her arm. She looks back at the train station as we start down the street, our shoes creaking in the snow. We pass dark shops that look like they haven't been open in long time. These are tough times, the war and all, but it shouldn't be this bad anywhere.

As we pass an apothecary, a small placard in the window catches my attention, and I pull up suddenly. Lera bumps into me and nearly falls, but I catch her arm and steady her back on her feet. I go back to the placard, a small yellowed rectangle with a simple but graceful squiggle on it, like a child's doodle. Most people wouldn't recognize it, but I do; it's the symbol used by The Order.

I peer through the window, but see no one inside the dark shop. I step back and look at the windows overtop the apothecary. The rooms upstairs are dark, like all the rooms in this city, it would appear.

"What's wrong?" Lera's voice is thin with tension. She huddles against the shop window, out of the falling snow.

"Nothing's wrong," I say, "but maybe some good luck for a change." I try the door, but it's locked, which comes as no surprise. I rap on the frame, but no one comes. Night has fallen, but with the blanket of white snow, it's still possible to see in the gloom. "Let's get out of the cold," I say. I feel exposed on the street. Once we secure a safe place for the night, we can return.

We start again down the street, and after another two blocks, we arrive at the Imperial Hotel, a stone building that disappears up into the night and falling snow. Like the other buildings, it's dark, but the front doors open when I pull on them. Lera hustles by me into the shadowy entryway before I can stop her. The closing door cuts off the windblown snow, which melts quickly into the entryway's slightly threadbare carpet. It takes several nervous seconds for my vision to adjust to the gloom, but in that moment, I push Lera behind me. My hand rests on the handle of my FP in its shoulder holster under my coat.

Slowly, dark shapes emerge from the blackness: chairs and sofas and small tables in a large open room. A hotel lobby. The furniture glows faintly in the yellow light of the small candle flickering on the top of an ornate reception desk ahead and to my right. My shoes click across the tiles, drawing a shadow from the dark rectangle of a door behind the desk.

"A foul night to be out," the shadow says.

I'm not in the mood for conversation. Already this mission has soured. I had expected to awaken tomorrow morning in Aurestapol. Now I will awaken in this dead town.

The desk attendant moves into the faint light. The yellow glow from the flame does nothing to give this sallow man's complexion a healthy color. His face is long and wrinkled, like melted candle wax and fringed with a wreath of fine gray hair. Patchy stubble peppers his chin, as if he's neglected his razor this week, but his suit coat is crisp, even if ill-fitting, and his tie is striped in the color of the Empire.

"Where is everyone?" I ask.

"In for the night, I would assume." He removes a ledger and opens it on the counter top. "You require a place to stay? Would that be one or two rooms?" He glances at Lera, who stands next to me, her back to the man.

"One room," I say.

"Of course."

I ignore his tone, which implies a false politeness in the presence of impropriety. "Why are all the buildings dark?" I ask, hoping a different question will draw an answer from the man.

He looks up from recording information in his guest ledger. "Trouble at the coal plant. Your name, sir."

"Petrenko. One night."

He hesitates for a moment, glancing up for a second before his pen scritches the name into the ledger.

"What sort of trouble?" I ask.

"I don't know," the attendant says, shrugging. He finishes with the ledger and closes it. Before he does, I notice several of the entries were for tonight and assume many of my fellow passengers have found their way here.

He takes my money and slips it into his coat pocket. From the same pocket he produces a heavy key. "The fourth floor. Last door at the end of the corridor. Do you require assistance with your baggage?"

"No. Is there a phone I can use?"

"I'm afraid the lines are down. They might have them fixed tomorrow, if the snow lets up."

"Is your kitchen open?"

"I'm sorry, but no. The kitchen is closed because of the trouble and with the snow, I can't get the help in. Maybe tomorrow morning."

I take the key from him, thanking him, even though he has been mostly unhelpful.

He nods acknowledgement and removes a candle

and holder from under the counter and lights the wick. He abandons it on the counter top and disappears through the door and leaving Lera and me alone in the empty lobby.

With the power out, the elevator isn't running, so we climb the stairs to the fourth floor. The key sticks in the lock, but with some manipulation, I get the door open then close and deadbolt it behind me. The room is small and crowded with a single bed, a pair of stiff-backed chairs and a writing desk. A telephone sits on the desk, but the earphone is silent, confirming what the desk clerk said.

The room is cold, but not uncomfortably so. I check the radiator. It's barely warm, but it should do for now.

The window looks out onto a narrow alley, and over the rooftop of the adjacent building, barely visible through the heavy snow and the darkness. I let the thick curtain fall back into place as much to hide the city as to hold in what warmth there is.

"What now?" Lera asks.

"We're going back to that apothecary," I say. "If we can find someone home, they might be able to help us."

"I don't want to go back in the snow," Lera says. "I'll keep the door locked and only open it for you."

I scan the room. The door is solid wood and the bolt looks strong. Without having to worry about her, I could get to the apothecary and back much faster.

"We can use a code word only you and me would know. Say 'winterhawk' when you come back, and I'll know it's you."

"Okay," I say. "Don't go anywhere. And stay away from the window. And keep the curtains closed."

She'll be safe here, I tell myself. No one knows we're in in St. Stephensburg and I'll be there and back in fifteen minutes.

She locks the door behind me, and the deadbolt clunks into place. The hallway is nearly pitch black, so I slide my hand against the wall as I head toward the stairs, counting off the doors as I go. Four rooms, then the landing to the stairs. I wind down to the first floor, cut through the dimly lit lobby, past a couple checking in at the desk, and out into the snow.

It's gotten colder.

The wind has piled the snow into drifts along the edge of the building, and lines of it snake along the pavement, driven by the city's odd eddies. I pluck my collar up straight to warm my neck and ears and lower my head into the wind and snow. By the time I arrive at the apothecary, my nose is red and running and ice crusts my eyebrows.

I cup my hands against the glass and peer in through the window. The shelves behind the long glass counter are empty, except for a few packages and bottles. Along the back wall, barely visible, is a door, presumably leading to a back room and likely stairs up to an apartment.

I try the door, but it's locked. I rap on the glass with my knuckle, quietly at first, but then harder when no one responds. After about a minute of knocking, the door on the back wall opens. A man sporting a neatly cropped van dyke, extends a stub of a candle and squints at me through the glass. He jabs a finger toward the sign hung in the door's window that clearly reads "closed."

In response, I point at the small placard with the symbol drawn on it.

The man's eyes widen. He fumbles with the lock on the door.

"Come in. Come in," he urges, stepping aside.

As I enter, the man brushes the snow from the shoulders of my coat. I stomp my feet on the doormat, dislodging caked snow from the soles of my shoes.

"You must be frozen," he says, still brushing away snow.

"The door," I say, and before I can say any more, he shuts and locks it.

"A night fit for dogs and horses," the man says, "not men of virtue and means."

The code—slightly modified to fit the situation but definitely the code—so I'm in the right place. Some of the tension in my shoulders eases.

"History shows men of virtue and means are always in short supply," I respond.

"You are with The Order," he says then, his surprise obvious. "I did not expect one would ever come to this place. I am Konstantin," he says, then shakes his head. "That is my cover in St. Stephensburg. It's been so long, it's as good as any other name, I guess."

I take his hand, but offer no name, which doesn't seem to bother Konstantin. He has a firm grip, and while he is a small man, who appears in middle years, he is muscular beneath the sleeves of his shirt. "I was en route to Aurestapol when my train was commandeered by the military."

"These are difficult times," Konstantin says.

"In some places more than others," I say, narrowing my eyes as I wonder if he will bite on my observation.

Konstantin grunts, but doesn't say anything else about it. Instead, he asks, "You were on the Trans-Sibirsk?"

What other train could it be? St. Stephensburg is a moderately-sized city and an important center for smelting raw iron, but how many passenger trains actually come through? It's one of the smaller stations on the Trans-Sibirsk line, and it's relatively isolated in the Central Range.

"From Olesk?"

"I need to contact Aurestapol."

"The lines are down," Konstantin says glumly.

"I was hoping you had a wireless."

He shakes his head. "This is a small outpost." He holds his hands, palms up, and shrugs meekly. Konstantin moves behind the counter and sets down the candle. "These are tough times. I don't have much at my disposal, but I can offer a room for the night."

"That won't be necessary," I say.

"You have a room at the Imperial?" He must see from my expression that his supposition is correct. "That is a comfortable place, and at least they still have regular heat and a functioning kitchen, even if the hours are limited."

"What's happened here?" I ask, my curiosity getting the best of me. Things are tough in Aurestapol—curfews and rationing, especially as the winter has worn on and the southern fronts have stagnated—but this is something more.

"Saboteurs," Konstantin says. "They damaged the rail lines, since repaired, but that has led to increased shortages in the city. Today something happened at the coal plant, so there's been no power since noon. Attacks on the smelting facilities … some unfortunate deaths."

"Papalate spies?"

"The worst kind," Konstantin says, grinning. He produces a half-empty bottle of vodka from beneath the counter, retrieves two medicine measuring cups from the nearly empty shelf then pours two fingers into each and slides one to me. "Also, I think, sympathizers. Those who would like to see the Empire injured or changed."

"I didn't know it was this bad," I say. News like this is controlled by the military, and I understand why. It is demoralizing to see strife in the Empire, more so with the current state of the war.

The vodka is low quality, but it burns a pleasant line of warmth through my chest. The contrast with the rest of my body sends a shiver through me.

"It's good?" Konstantin pours himself another glass, having finished the first.

"The saboteurs ... Silver Tigers?" I ask, wanting to bring the conversation back.

Konstantin shrugs. "I don't know that name, but if you think so, then probably. They hide in the mountains, where the soldiers can't find them, and sometimes shell the city at night. Tonight, though, too much snow, so it is safe."

Even though it is cold inside the shop, the snow has melted off my long coat. The ice in my eyebrows has turned into the droplets that I wipe as they run down the side of my face.

"I need to get to Aurestapol," I say. I've decided I don't want to spend a minute more in this town than I need to. "Do you have a vehicle that can make that trip?"

Konstantin's lips curl into a surprised oh-shape.

"Aurestapol is far, especially with the snow. Even under the best conditions, I wouldn't trust most autos to make that distance. That's a lot of empty land, and you'll be pressed to find open spin stations along the way."

Perhaps Konstantin is right, and we should sit tight in St. Stephensburg until the next train. No one knows we're here.

Konstantin smooths his beard. "I have a motorbike fully spun up. If the snow stops …"

I shake my head. "I need something for two."

"Hrm, something for two." Konstantin taps his temple as he concentrates. "I think—yes, I think I can help you. Wait here while I get my coat." He tops off my glass before disappearing through the door into the back.

While I wait for him to return, I look out the window at the dark city and the heavy snow. If the weather doesn't break, there is no way, auto or not, we'll be leaving. St. Stephensburg is on the western flank of the central mountains, but we would still need to travel across rough ground before reaching the flatlands of the western Empire. I'm not sure any vehicle could make progress under these conditions.

At least if we're stuck in the city for the night, the risk of being shelled is low. A silver lining, I try to convince myself. A shame they have not been able to catch the insurgents. Politically I don't know what the rebels hope to accomplish by terrorizing the populace. It's a self-defeating tactic, it seems, unless the primary purpose is to increase the suffering in the hopes that Empire will begin to take the blame for not protecting the people. I can see how that could weaken the power of the government, but it would never allow those responsible to take power. The people upon whom they perpetrated the hardship would never accept them, but a rival faction could take advantage of the power vacuum. I can think of no one that could do that, but then, I had heard nothing of the Silver Tigers until a few days ago.

Why am I only learning about this now? I know I am only a loyal foot soldier, working only a small, and usually foreign, corner of this vast maze, but the insurrectionists seem important. Until this day, I have always assumed the violence within our borders has been perpetrated by isolated Papalate spies. Or, more accurately, I had been led to believe that. Now it appears to be more than that, and these Silver Tigers are at the heart of it. The Silver Tigers seem to be everywhere. Aurestapol. Olesk. Maybe here in St. Stephensburg.

I have lost sight of the city outside, and so instead track the falling snow in a near-hypnotic trance.

I need to get back to Aurestapol.

Where is Konstantin?

I turn back to the empty shop room, which has grown colder during the past few minutes—cold enough that I now see my breath hanging in a cloud before my eyes. The door into the back room is ajar. As I approach, cold air streaming through the crack sets my candle flame dancing. I cup the candle with my free hand to save it from going out.

With the toe of my boot, I push the door open.

The light barely pushes through the gloom into the narrow corridor. To my right, a flight of stairs goes up. To the left, a door has blown open, leaving a skirt of snow on the floorboards of the hallway. The wind gutters the flame to a low blue stub, and blows up under my jacket, sending a fierce chill shuddering up my spine.

I realize almost too late that the chill is not from the wind only, but–

I throw myself against the far wall as a throwing knife sinks into the doorframe where my chest had been a second before. The candle topples from its holder and goes out, casting the hallway into pitch blackness.

Heavy footsteps pound the stairs. I spin just in time to face my assailant and deflect him from leaping fully onto me. He lands next to me at the bottom of the stairs. My vision, not yet adjusted to the darkness, is useless. As I raise my arms to defend my face, a blade slices through the sleeve of my long coat, but only nicks my skin. I slap the hand away, trying to buy myself moments, but my assailant, who has the build of Konstantin and smells of cheap vodka, is on me again.

I duck and the knife hits the wall. I slip under Konstantin's arm and behind him, and strike his knee with my boot. The limb crumples. Konstantin cries out in pain as he teeters backward. Seizing his shirt, I thrust him downward, driving his head into the stairs. The dark body twitches once and stops moving. I nudge the dark lump with my boot, and it slides limply down a step, but does not otherwise move.

I strike a match and set it to the candle stub. Konstantin is slumped awkwardly on his side on the steps, and leaking blood from the wound onto the stairs. I doubt he'll be waking any time soon, if at all. I notice above the collar of his shirt, a patch of dark skin. Pulling the collar down, I find the same mark as on the assassin in Aurestapol and Dai Lei in Olesk.

Konstantin isn't with The Order.

I look quickly up the steps, wondering if I'm still in immediate danger, but nothing feels wrong. I draw my FP and creep upstairs to a loft apartment with a high ceiling that the candlelight barely reaches. On the round kitchen table is a bottle of vodka and a platter of smoked fish, roe, and cheese slices. The bottle of vodka is nearly empty and two tall glasses sit opposite each other.

So where is Konstantin's friend?

Sweat trickles down my back as I squint into the darkness. I feel exposed carrying the candle, like I'm spotlighted for a shooter, but nothing can be done about that. I edge around so I can see behind table into the kitchen area of the large open room. A rat scuttles across the floor, frightening me enough that I nearly shoot it. It scurries into a hole beneath the sink.

"Where are you, little friend," I whisper.

I pull the closet door open, but find only a table and shortwave radio hooked to a hand-crank generator. The top of the unit is warm to the touch; it's been used recently, probably during the past ten minutes considering the temperature in the apartment.

There is no sign of Konstantin's friend, and that feels like an icicle in my gut.

The back door.

I run down the steps and out the still ajar back door, taking care not to fall in the snow in the hallway. The wind nearly blows out my candle, but I keep it lit with a hand around the flame. The narrow alley into which the door opens is empty, and it's too dark to see very far. Footprints, half-filled from the falling snow, vanish off into the dark.

I curse my stupidity. I had let my guard down because he had known the code, but codes can be stolen.

The footprints head off in the direction of the Imperial Hotel.

The flame goes out as I drop the candle into the snow and run.

I fall several times, and by the time I reach the hotel, my long coat and trousers are caked with snow and my hands are raw-red. I leave a trail of ice on the carpet as I circle the perimeter of the lobby, keeping my back to the wall and my FP raised. The lobby is empty. I pause to listen for footsteps, but my breathing is so heavy from running that I need to hold my breath to hear anything.

Silence presses on my ears.

The door behind the counter is still open, a faint light flickering from within. I edge around the counter and stop. The desk clerk is face down on the floor. Blood shimmers like wine in the candlelight. A widening circle seeps from flechette wounds in his neck and shoulders.

The shots were placed by a professional to kill quickly and quietly–the wounds would have perforated his larynx, making it impossible for him to scream, and then severed the arteries. Given the amount of blood, I estimate he was shot less than two minutes ago.

I'm dealing with a trained killer. Lera won't stand a chance if he knows what room she's in.

I can only hope the desk attendant didn't tell him. The drawer where he stored his ledger is partially open, the ledger gone. The pit in my stomach gets colder. He knows what rooms are occupied, and if he works from the bottom of the list–

I run, taking the stairs two at a time. One person checked in after us; I recall the elderly couple chatting with the attendant as I was leaving. I pray their room is on the top floor.

The carpet runner on the stairs muffles the sound of my feet. Up I charge, each of the floors empty as far as I can tell, but I'm moving so quickly and each corridor is so dark I can't say anything with certainty. I reach the fourth floor, pitch black, like a mineshaft. My fingers drag down the wall. One door, two, three, four, and I stop.

"Lera," I whisper hoarsely, but she doesn't answer. I find it hard to speak. After running back from the shop and up four flights of stairs, I'm winded. Nervously I look back toward the stairs. "Lera, open the door," I say again, this time a little louder.

An eternity seems to pass. Finally the bolt grinds as it slides aside. I push on the door and it yanks suddenly to a stop on the chain.

"You didn't say the password," Lera says.

"Open the damn door."

She must hear the urgency in my voice because she doesn't argue. The door closes for a second as she releases the chain.

I slip quickly into the room and wrench the bolt back into place.

"I'm sorry," Lera says. "I was just–"

"We've got to go," I say in a rush of breath, her foolish game now forgotten. The adrenaline coursing through me leaves my hands and knees jittery, but I know they'll respond when called upon.

"What's happening?"

"We have to leave. We've been found."

As if I prodded her with a red-hot stick, Lera jumps back from me. She bumps into the chair and writing desk, nearly knocking herself off her feet. I grab her arm, shushing her, and she falls quiet.

I put my finger to my mouth, creep back over to the door, and put my ear lightly to the wood. Silence in the hallway, but with all the carpet, it's impossible to know if anyone is out there. The assassin could be standing on the other side of the door, listening, for all I know.

My mouth is dry, but the handle of my FP is slick in my hand. I wipe my palm on my trouser leg and ready myself by wedging my boot against the bottom edge of the door. I motion to Lera to step out of the line of sight. She blows out the candle and moves to her left.

The bolt is cool against my fingers. I wince as it grumbles, metal on metal, but the door isn't forced open.

Lera comes up behind me.

The knob turns easily, and I crack the door wide enough to peer out into dark hallway. As I'm about to step out, a light comes down the stairs and a man in a heavy jacket and a thick cap of curly hair steps into the corridor. I duck back into the room and close the door. I'm afraid to slide the bolt, because of the noise it will make.

"The window," I whisper.

I peel back the curtain. Cold wind and snow flood in as I heave the window open. Lera turns away from the blowing snow.

I grab her arm before she can retreat. "It's time to be brave, okay?"

She takes a deep breath to gather her courage. Swinging her leg out, she squeezes through the opening onto the fire escape.

I follow her out.

Lera presses against the wall to my left, her feet on the only snowless patch of grating.

"Not down," I say. We won't reach the bottom before the assassin gets here and he's skilled enough that we would be easy targets. We could go up, but he would see our footsteps in the snow.

A narrow ledge, not more than two hands in width, runs along the wall at the height of the windowsill. Given its narrowness, it's sheltered from the falling snow and almost devoid of ice. The ledge disappears into the darkness.

"Onto the ledge," I say.

"The ledge?"

I hoist her up onto the ledge next to the window. Instinctively she flattens her back against the wall. I climb up next to her and grab her hand. A gust of wind whips at my long coat, nearly unbalancing me. I press my back to the wall. Good thing it's dark, and I can't see the ground or I would lose my nerve, but it's too late to do anything else.

I squeeze Lera's hand. "Everything is going to be okay," I say, not sure if she hears me or if my words are whipped away by the wind.

I start along the ledge, gently forcing Lera ahead of me. I fight against my instinct to move slowly and cautiously. In my mind, I see the assassin, a faceless form with frizzy hair at the door to our room. Perhaps he's knocked, assuming Lera would not suspect anything. Maybe he hasn't and instead is trying the knob to see if, by some miracle, the door is not locked.

Keep moving … keep moving. I can't control the assassin, so I focus on something I can control.

My shoes slide across the stone work–the scraping reaches my ears every time the wind lets up. I make the mistake of looking down at my feet. My toes hang over the edge, and the knowledge that I'm four stories up is enough to set my head spinning. I gasp and press against the stone wall behind me. I feel as if I'm falling, even though the stone is solid against my back.

Lera's hand is squeezing the feeling from my fingers. She stares straight off into the night, her jaw clenched tightly. Even with the dark, her face is pale as the moon.

She's not wearing her cloak and I curse the oversight, but there's no going back for it. We need to keep moving. Any second the assassin will look out the window, and I hope he decides we either went up or down the fire escape.

That hope spurs me on, and I continue along the ledge. We should reach another window soon. I look back; the fire escape has vanished into the darkness and the snow. "Don't move," I whisper.

A clang comes out of the darkness as the assassin steps out the window and onto the fire escape. I raise my FP, but given the precariousness of our position, I don't want to risk a shot unless we are discovered. I hold my breath. It's cold, but I'm covered in sweat. The seconds it takes for the assassin to decide what we've done stretch to eternity, with only the silence of the snowfall and the dark, punctuated by bursts of wind in my ears. My mouth moves in silent prayer, urging the assassin to go down or up, and not to look too hard along the ledge because I don't believe we've gone far enough to be entirely hidden.

The silence continues as he weighs his options, but if he's a professional, he will make a decision soon– the sound of footsteps clangs down the fire escape ladder.

And I can breathe again, a column of mist expelled as the danger moves away from us.

We have bought a minute at least. He will likely figure out his error when he reaches the ground and searches through the snow for footprints. Finding none, he will likely come back up to the room and continue his search. We need to be away before that happens.

I squint into the darkness. Ahead I see the window into the next room. We have to hurry, not only because the assassin will be back, but because my feet and hands are going numb in the cold. Without her cloak, Lera must be even colder than me. I gently push her forward again, and we inch along the ledge, over an icy patch where one of the hotel's downspouts has leaked, and reach the window.

She reaches down to pull it open and nearly loses her balance. Lera grabs my elbow, and it's just enough for her to regain herself.

"It's locked," she says. Her teeth chatter loudly, making her difficult to understand.

I hand her my FP. "Break the top pane and reach in and unlock it."

She takes the pistol barrel and taps the pane on the upper window. The glass breaks, but doesn't entirely shatter. The pieces fall inside and are caught in the lining of the thick curtains, which muffle the noise.

"Hurry," I say.

She reaches through the hole and releases the latch then pulls up the window and carefully slides inside. I follow, wincing as glass crunches under my feet. Thankfully, the room is empty.

Lera is nearly frozen and stands shivering in her dress. I'm amazed she has been able to stand out in the cold as long as she has. I remove my long coat and wrap it around her shoulders, and she holds it tightly around her neck with a pale, trembling hand. Shivers wrack her body.

I crack the door.

The door to our room is closed. We sprint down the hallway to the stairs, Lera tight on my heels.

"Who was that?" she asks, but I hush her.

The stairs fly under us, our footsteps muffled on the carpet runner–around and around the landings, until we reach the ground floor where I stop. I peer out into the lobby. It's empty, lit only by the faint flicker of the candle on the counter.

We hustle across to the exit. Outside the door, Lera reflexively pulls up short before the falling snow. I tug her arm, and she follows, but she hugs the building wall, staying out of the snowfall as well as she can. She thrusts her arms into the sleeves of my jacket and ties the belt securely to keep it closed. The collar, once pulled up, is high enough to nearly cover her entire face, and the bottom of my coat dredges through the drifting snow on the sidewalk.

We turn away from the alley and move quickly in the opposite direction.

"Who was that?" Lera asks again, nearly jogging to stay on my hip.

Without breaking stride, I look over my shoulder. The entrance to the Imperial Hotel has already fallen into the darkness, but I don't slow.

Lera tugs my arm, bringing us to halt. "Who was that?"

"I don't know," I say, "but they didn't have our best interests in mind." It's the truth. "This isn't the time for questions. Let's get out of here while we can." We start up the street again.

"Where are we going?"

"I don't know yet."

"We can't walk to Aurestpol," she says.

"I'm aware of that," I say, biting back stronger words. "Keep walking, and be quiet so I can think."

We go another block, but even with the Imperial Hotel lost in the snow behind us, I don't feel any better. In truth, my stomach is sour, likely as much from nerves and adrenaline as it is from hunger. The sweat that has soaked through my shirt makes me cold, and my suit coat isn't thick enough to keep me warm for long. The handle of the FP is icy enough to numb my fingers.

Even if properly dressed, we're not safe on the street. Our footprints won't fill fast enough if our pursuer has any skills. He might be two blocks behind us right now. If he knows the city, he might already be a block in front of us. Running blindly through the streets makes no sense, so I pull Lera into a door alcove to get us out of the blowing snow while I think. Tucked into the shadows, we can't be seen easily from the street, but our footprints betray us. There's nothing I can do about that, however.

"We'll freeze if we stay out here," Lera says.

I shiver violently as if to punctuate her statement.

"We could hide in one of these buildings." She quietly rattles the doorknob near her waist, but it's locked.

Hiding in St. Stephensburg isn't the answer. With the rate the snow is accumulating, we could be trapped here with our assassin for several days. He knows the city and maybe has friends, and access to more weapons supplies. All we have is my FP and single coat between us.

I don't like those odds.

No, we need to get out of St. Stephensburg.

My shivering is getting worse, and I wonder how it will affect my talent. Often, a shiver is the first indication that something is about to go wrong. As far as my instincts are concerned, every shiver now is a false alarm, but I know eventually, one won't be, and I wonder if I'd recognize it for what it truly is and react in time.

I peer out of the alcove, but I see nothing through the heavy snow and darkness. "If only we knew where he was," I say through chattering teeth. "Come on."

As I step out of the alcove, a violent shiver rocks me, and my head spins. Without hesitation, I push Lera back into shadow. I shove in next to her, shushing her protests. We're as far back into the shadows as we can get, but our breath, hanging in a fog, is silver in the faint snow-light.

I hold my breath.

The falling snow hasn't filled our footprints, but enough has collected to take the sharp edges from them.

I position my body so Lera is behind me. I hold my FP in both hands because I'm afraid I'll drop it if I hold it with only one.

Seconds tick by, marked by the fat flakes fluttering

down through the night. Ten seconds ... fifteen. My head is getting light.

I exhale slowly, draw in an equally slow breath, but still no one appears.

I lean forward, afraid that if I take a step the snow will creak under my shoes, and peer around the alcove edge. Less than twenty meters away, a dark shape stands at the intersection through which we just passed, studying the snowy ground. It's hard to see him clearly; the only feature I can distinguish is a fuzzy afro of dark curls. It's the same man as at the hotel. He reaches a decision and continues down the street without turning toward us.

"We have to move," I say. It likely will take only a few seconds for our pursuer to realize he's gone the wrong way and double back.

We step out into the snow and continue down the street away from the intersection, moving quickly. We pass the dark hump of a parked auto, and I try the door, but it's locked. A half block later we pass another, but its doors are also locked. I could break the window, but that would make a lot of noise, and we'd end up freezing to death before we got two kilometers down the street.

We stop at the next intersection, but seeing no one in the crossroad, we sprint across. For the next few minutes we move quickly. I have no plan, turning whenever I see an auto on a side street. They are all locked. My hand gets so cold, I drop my weapon. After the second time, I shove my FP into my shoulder holster and try to warm my hands in my suit coat pockets.

Soon, I'm hopelessly turned around, and I stop when we come to an auto whose door handle has had the snow knocked off it. I'm so cold, it takes me a moment to realize what this means—we've been here before.

I scan the street for any signs of our pursuer, certain that he must be nearby. It's only a matter of time before he finds us or we stumble stupidly across his path. Then it will be over. Cold and disoriented, I find myself paralyzed into inaction.

"Let's go back to the hotel," Lera says. She's shivering too, leaving me wondering how long we've been out here.

"No, not back there," I say. If unable to find us, I would expect him to return to the Imperial because it's one of the few places we know in St. Stephensburg, and he might reasonably expect us to return there. We can't stay on the street without freezing to death.

A particularly strong shiver spasms through me, and Lera yelps as I pull her down behind the auto. My teeth chatter so loudly that if our pursuer is anywhere nearby he'll hear.

"You'll lose your fingers if we stay out her much longer," Lera says.

True, I can't feel my fingers, and my toes are lumps at the end of my feet. "He could be anywhere," I say, more to myself than to Lera. "Anywhere."

"What if you knew where he was?"

I stare at her, not comprehending.

Snow crusts her bangs. "I can find him," she says, softly.

"You can what?" My ears are so cold, I'm not sure I heard her right.

Lera sighs heavily, shaking her head. "Hold these," she says, peeling off her goggles. The water held inside splashes down the front of the long coat. She blinks several times, as if the cold air stings her eyes. She crouches forward, supporting herself on her hands. Several deep breaths create a low fog. She pushes her face into the ankle-deep snow.

I draw back. I'm not sure why, but the sight of her face down in the snow disconcerts me. I'm not put at ease when she starts shaking, and her breathing becomes ragged. I want to pull her head out of the snow, but I'm afraid to touch her. Her shaking increases, and it looks as if she has started to convulse. When I grab her shoulder, she tumbles over onto her back. Her face is white and snow clings to her wide-open eyes.

"Lera? Lera?" I repeat her name, more desperately each time, but she doesn't respond.

As I pull her into my arms, I realize I'm too weak to pick her up, so I hold onto her instead. Her shaking eases and her breathing becomes steadier. She blinks at me.

"Are you okay?" I ask.

She tries to say something, but it takes her several attempts. Finally, she points down the street in the direction we had just come and says, "He's a block away … he's coming."

"Can you walk?" We have to flee; in my condition, I can't fight him.

Lera nods. "My goggles. Pack them with snow…"

I do as she says as quickly as I can, and help her pull them over her eyes.

"Can you see?"

"Well enough," she says. "Damn, that's cold."

We get to our feet, and I'm immediately more concerned about me than her. I can barely stand my feet are so numb, but together we stumble up the street back in the general direction of the Imperial Hotel. Looking back, I think I see someone a block behind us, but the snow is heavy, so I can't be certain. At the first intersection, we turn away from the hotel.

I push us on onward, faster. If he was close enough for me to see him, then he could have seen us. Ahead, a parked auto is covered in a skin of snow. I try the door and find it unlocked. "In here."

I push her in and follow on her heels, carefully pulling closed the door behind me. We're jammed into the passenger seat, a tangle of limbs. Her elbow stabs into my kidneys.

"Stay down," I hiss when she tries to move.

Our breath fills the interior with vapor. I strain to hear our pursuer, and pray he doesn't notice the snow knocked off the door. Piled into the auto as we are, I can't duck beneath the level of the window, but it's very dark.

A shadow goes by.

I still don't move and force myself to count to ten. No more; no less.

"Let's get out of here."

Lera squeaks something that I take to be agreement. I ignore her protests as I twist around and pull myself over the stick shift into the driver's seat. With some effort, I get straightened behind the wheel.

Now alone in the passenger seat, Lera straightens.

It's a newer auto, I notice now. I check the dashboard and curse. A steering lock.

"I need a thin piece of metal," I say.

Lera reaches up to her hair and removes one of her barrettes. "Will this work?"

My hands are so numb I can't handle the barrette.

After I nearly drop it, Lera takes it from me. "Tell me what to do."

I instruct her to fold the metal clip back on itself to open it up into a flat strip less than the width of my pinky. While she does this, I try to rub heat back into my hands, but the inside of the auto isn't any warmer than outside in the snow. "Perfect," I say when Lera finishes. The next part is tricky, so I carefully take the metal from her. I concentrate on my fingers, watching them close around the barrette before I'm convinced I have it. I guide the tip into the key slot. I need to force it, but the metal slides in. I blow more warm air onto my fingers, but still there's no feeling. "Here's to some good luck for a change," I say. I rotate the metal and the steering wheel comes free as the lock disengages. I grin as I press the starter button and the dash lights up.

"It started!" Lera says. "You did it."

"We did it."

The flywheel is at three-quarter spin and the batteries are low, but it'll have to do.

I turn on the wipers and wait for them to push aside the snow. There's no heater, but Lera finds a pair of leather gloves on the dash, and I put them on. It's been a long time since I've driven an auto, and my fingers tightly grip the wheel. I feel around for the lights, but don't turn them on–the city is dark and quiet, and I wonder if I should risk attracting any attention. I squint through the windshield and realize I have no choice. I can't see anything. I turn on the headlamps, but still can see only a few meters into the falling snow.

I pull the stick into gear and the engine whines as

the flywheel engages the drive shaft. Shuddering, the vehicle creeps forward. I have no idea where I'm going, but I need to find a road west. We wander through town, up and down dark snowy streets. I'm afraid that any moment we'll run into our pursuer, but our luck holds.

"We're lost," Lera says, her voice hushed and edged with uncertainty, fear.

It's the truth, even if I don't want to give it life by giving it words. I'm thankful when Lera doesn't say any more about it.

Round and round, we circle the buildings, which all look alike. The snow continues to fall, drifting in the street and getting deeper. The auto's tires crunch through, but the handling is deteriorating, and I'm starting to fear we won't get out of St. Stephensburg. Even if we do, how far will we get? I'm wasting precious spin wandering blindly through the dark streets, but I don't know what else to do. We can't stay here, so I continue to drive, circling down dark avenues until by chance I happen to recognize the train station.

We skid to a stop as I crunch the brake.

I lower the window because the glass is fogged up. After a moment studying the area, I get my bearings. I recall the direction of the tracks and know which way to go. I roll up the window and begin to drive again.

We slowly pick our way through the city, the headlamps reflecting off the falling snow. We can barely move faster than a running person, but we make progress. The tall buildings gradually give way to squat tenements and narrow lanes.

Lera stares out the window, chewing nervously at a

finger. The light from the dash plays over her face. Her jaw is tight. The snow in her goggles has melted, and the water sloshes around at the level of her eyebrows. I wonder what she can see.

"What happened back there in the snow? You saw him." On the train she had said she sees through water lenses, but I thought she meant like a normal person would see through glass. This was something more.

"You could see everyone," I say. I try to sound certain, but it really is a question. "Everyone in contact with the snow."

She stops chewing on her finger, and hides her hand in her lap as if suddenly self-conscious. "Yes, I saw everyone." She looks away from me.

This talent could change the tide of the war. She could see across an entire battlefield and know the location of every enemy soldier. If she could identify specific soldiers, say those in command, we could cut off the head of the enemy with a series of surgical strikes. We could end the war.

The implications take my breath way.

"How did you know it was him?" I ask.

She's trembling. The color is gone from her face, but I don't know if it's a trick of the dashboard glow.

"How did you know?" I ask again, as gently as possible so she doesn't think I'm interrogating her.

"I just knew."

"It's more than that, isn't it?"

She turns away and looks out the window.

I know what she's going through. I've lived this moment. There was a time when I was afraid to tell anyone about my talent. After being teased, beaten, and called a liar, I had stopped talking about it. I had hidden it, buried it, and disowned it as best I could. My talent was my dirty secret. Only later did I learn I wasn't alone, and that others understood. I know that now that my talent is a gift, but when I was Lera's age, it was only a curse.

I wonder how many times someone made her cry. How many times they left her bruised. How many times she shed her blood and tears and pain into the quiet dark at night, hoping none of the other children in the dorm would hear her sobbing into her pillow. If my life was any measure, more times than anyone deserves.

"I get premonitions of violence and danger," I say. "It's what The Order calls a talent. A special skill, like your vision. When I was eight, I went to an orphanage, I told one of the boys about my premonitions, but he called me a liar, and when I persisted, a freak. He and another boy jumped me that afternoon in the brickyard and beat me bloody. 'Guess you didn't see that coming,' he said when they were finished. But I had seen it; the moment I had walked around the corner into the brickyard, but I had already decided being a liar was better than being a freak.

"But we're not freaks. Someday you'll understand that and accept your talent for what it is: a gift."

"No," she says. "You can't understand at all." Her voice is strained, and she's shaking visibly now. "What you do, your talent or whatever, saves your life. Mine destroys me because I don't just see people, I see *into* people. I see their all fear and their hate. I see the deepest, darkest core of what they are, and I see it for every single person who is in contact with me.

"I knew it was him because I could taste his hate and fear. I could smell it. I could see it. I could feel it, right to his rotten core. I could feel everyone's. Everyone's!" And she's looking at me now, those white, white eyes drilling into me through those watery lenses.

Can she see into me again even though only air separates us? If she could, she would see remorse, not fear. Well, to be honest, she'd see fear too.

My brow crinkles.

All my life, I suspected people feared me because of my talent. That's what drove the boys in the orphanage to beat me up. They weren't jealous of me; they feared me. I may know this to be true, but I never *felt* it.

Everyone has fears. It's the most basic of human emotions, the most visceral, and her talent is she sees it; she feels it, and tonight she lived the fear of everyone in the snows of St. Stephensburg. How many people was that? It couldn't have been many, but however many it was, it nearly overwhelmed her. How many would it take to break her?

That is why she's afraid. She doesn't know either. One of these times she uses her talent, she could be overwhelmed to the point that she might never recover.

"You're right," I say. "I can't understand. I'm sorry; I didn't know."

We ride on in silence. The squat buildings and narrow lanes give way to open lots carpeted in snow. Holding the wheel is painful, as my hands are pierced with sharp pins and needles. I take this as a good sign that I won't lose any fingers. After an hour of slow progress, we are driving along a snowy track visible only because of the snow-laden conifers that line it. The last of my adrenaline drains away, and I'm suddenly tired.

Lera snores quietly in the seat next to me.

Asleep, she looks at peace, but how long will that peace last? The Order wants her for her talent, but if she continues to use her talent, eventually, no matter how carefully, something bad will happen.

PART III

OCKHAM'S RAZOR

WE WIND DOWN THE VALLEY, a river on our right, frozen mostly, except where the land drops and the riffles can tumble, creating enough noise that I hear it over the whir of the engine. The train track runs along the river edge, but it's buried in snow as well as shrouded in the dark.

Going steadily downhill allows me to ease off the accelerator and conserve spin. Even so, we aren't going to make it far; the auto's three-flywheel array is better suited for short distance travel and Aurestapol is at least a day away by train.

Two hours later, we reach the valley floor and the land widens. We've come down out of the falling snow, and the road is a clear dark line through stark white fields. The engine whir increases as I accelerate.

A few farmhouses slide by in the night–dark shadows resting on snow-covered fields like hibernating marmots. One of these farms could likely re-spin our vehicle, but I don't want to risk an encounter unless I absolutely have to. Fortunately, after another twenty minutes we arrive at a small cluster of buildings on a crossroad, and I pull into a shuttered spin station. I pound on the door, but no one answers; the proprietor must not live on the property.

"What now?" Lera stands next to me in the cold, stomping her feet.

I find a jack handle in the boot, and pry open the charging bay door. Other than a single loud pop as the latch breaks, it doesn't make much noise, and no lights come on in the other buildings. I plug the power lead in, and flip the switch on the battery bank, hoping the station has been fully charged. Lights wink to life on the panel.

Lera sighs audibly.

It'll take about an hour to fully spin-charge the auto, but that will still leave several hours of darkness.

"Get back inside," I say. "No sense freezing out here."

"You coming?" she asks when I don't move to follow.

"I'm going to keep watch out here for a while."

She gives me back my long coat. The sleeves are warm and the collar smells faintly of cheap soap. It takes me nearly half an hour to get comfortably warm, and then I get steadily colder again over the next forty minutes as I wait for the auto to finish re-spinning. I disconnect the power lead and leave enough money to pay for the re-spin and the broken lock.

Then we're on the road again, driving west into the night.

The inside of the auto grows humid and warm from our body heat. Lera snores softly in the seat next to me, but I'm alert, scanning the road behind me for headlamps. I've seen no indication that the assassin, or anyone else, has followed us out of St. Stephensburg, but I can't relax, especially as this is the only road to our final destination, and it's likely only a matter of time before someone comes looking for us. Or maybe they already have agents awaiting us in the towns ahead.

I'm used to danger, but this is something different. I'm not even sure if they are after me or Lera. I play the events of St. Stephensburg over, searching for clues, but finding nothing that helps me understand the motivations of my pursuers. The simplest explanation is the Silver Tigers–if that's who they are– are after agents of The Order, but I've learned the world is often more complicated than Ockham would have us believe, and the simplest explanation doesn't always cut to the core of a problem. I console myself with the reality that at this moment I don't need to understand my pursuers's motivations; that knowledge doesn't change the treacherous road ahead. Someone is trying to kill or capture me or Lera or both of us, and I cannot allow that to happen.

When dawn comes, we are in the mouth of the valley under a thick cloud pack that diffuses the light from the rising sun. The road straightens and rolls over a series of gentle ridges and folds in the land before dropping onto the western plain. A straight road and a day of driving to reach Aurestapol stretches before us.

We drive on for another hour until the spin on the flywheel is again nearly spent. We stop at a spin station in a nothing town in the middle of nowhere. While they spin-charge the auto, Lera and I buy borscht and bread from the elderly woman in the attached shop. The borscht is salty, the slices of rye bread slightly stale, but it's hot and fills our empty stomachs.

Lera says nothing while we eat, and the awkward silence sits between us like the earthy smell of the beets. I don't know what to say, so I say nothing; instead I keep watch out the window, but no autos pass on the road.

By the time we finish, our auto is spin-charged, and we continue onward. After several more hours, I'm growing tired of staring at the monotonous white fields the stretch to the horizon in every direction. The danger of St. Stephensburg feels so many miles and hours away. When I ask, Lera tells me she doesn't know how to drive, so I crack the window, squeeze the wheel, and drive on.

A few yawns later, I ask her to talk to me.

She tells me about the orphanage and the kindly Mrs. Okimoto. They are familiar stories. Her feelings of worthlessness as other children were always adopted instead of her, and the eventual realization that the chances anyone would ever want her decreasing with each passing birthday. The whispers of the younger children; their sorry looks as they, too, know her fate. Finally she tells me about the day when Mrs. Okimoto told her that someone wanted her.

"It's strange," she says, almost wistfully, "all I ever wanted was to leave that place, but when it finally happened, I didn't want go. It was not ever a happy place, but it was the only place I ever knew."

I nod knowingly. I remember that same day– Mistress Markov telling me the night before that she had found a place for me. I learned later that she hadn't found me a family, but that The Order had found me. I was seventeen, scrawny, and scared of my own shadow. The other boys made a sport of terrorizing me. Yet as I got into the auto that had been sent to take me away, I remember looking back at that dreary brick building with the bars on the windows, and feeling a knot in my stomach. Sometimes what we know, no matter how bad it might be, is less scary than something we don't know. I was lucky; The Order turned out well for me.

That's not always the case for everyone.

SEVERAL MORE HOURS PASS. Several more spin
stations, all shuttered and desolate in the snowy quiet,
slide by. When the wind gusts, the auto trembles. The
auto's spin winds down with my alertness, and as the
afternoon grows old, I worry about both.

At a crossroad, we pass an ice-rimed sign for
Novirsk, still many kilometers away down the narrow
side lane, and something clicks in my head. I nearly
dismiss it, but I don't have the luxury to be picky.

Working from a decade-old memory, I turn
around and take the lane toward Novirsk.

Lera gives me a questioning look.

"We need to re-spin," I say. "And rest. I know of a
place not far from here where I think we can do
both."

The narrow lane winds off between empty, snowy
fields, boxed off with low stone walls. The sober,
treeless land, shades of gray and white and blue, rolls
off unbroken into obscurity. Wind moves the snow
around, blurring the distance. The way the gray sky
glows, it's impossible to see the horizon; the land

seems to curve right up and over our heads and back down onto the other side of the road, like we're trapped in a snow globe.

The warning indicator winks at me on the dash.

After another quarter hour, we come to a stone archway over a narrow snow-packed track that winds off to the east. I turn into the lane, passing under the archway into which the name "Bragin" is carved.

I get a hole in my stomach, and I nearly turn the auto around, but we'd never make it back to the crossroad.

Lera blinks her large eyes at me. "What is this place?"

"Bragin Manor," I say. "I used to know the person who lives here."

"*Used* to know?"

"I haven't seen her in over a decade. We didn't part under the best circumstances." I'm not sure why I feel the need to tell Lera that last bit. It just comes out, and I'm struck at how inadequately the words explain what happened.

"Her? Did you leave her at the altar or something?"

"Not exactly."

Lera's lips curl into a surprised o-shape.

My ears grow hot, and I focus on the road.

The narrow lane, lined with short evergreen hedges, goes straight off toward the horizon, and soon I see the house in the distance—a block of dark stone. As we draw nearer, it becomes apparent the house is dark, but I can't tell if thick curtains have been drawn or the place has been abandoned. Bragin Manor is a two-story edifice, with wide stone stairs that sweep up to a set of impressive doors that wouldn't look out of place on a castle gate. Windows with elaborate scroll-work iron bars make two neat rows to either side of the doors. The drive circles in front of the house before looping around to the back and the carriage house.

I stop the auto and disengage the drive shaft. My fingers shake, and I grip the wheel to hide it.

The cold air hits me like a fist when I step out of the auto. It hurts to draw a breath, and it feels like my nose has frozen solid in an instant. Lera covers her mouth with her hand, but I see that she, too, is struggling to catch a breath after the warm, humid air inside the auto.

"Goodness, it's cold," she says, trying to burrow her head into my long coat.

Up close, the house looks deserted. The shutters on the window are weathered and several hang askew. One of the drainage pipes is missing its lower half; a large icicle extends down the side of the house to the ground. The snow on the landing is deep enough to cover my shoes and is undisturbed.

I lift the knocker on the door and let it fall.

I've only been outside a few seconds, but already I'm shivering and the metal door knocker is cold enough to burn my fingers.

Several seconds pass. I pound the knocker a second time.

Lera turns away from the wind, and says something, but my ears are throbbing from the cold. She heads back towards the auto.

I try the knocker a third time. My fingers grow numb.

The wind whips the snow around my ankles. I can't take it any longer, and start to turn back to the auto. I'll drive around back and check if the spin-charger in the carriage house is still working. I stop when the door bolt clicks. When I turn back, the door is cracked and a rifle muzzle points at me through the narrow opening.

I put my hands up. "Odella?"

The rifle doesn't move. I squint into the darkness where I can see only a bulky shadow in the narrow gap—a heavy coat and hat, and maybe a scarf wrapped around the face, but it's hard to tell in the darkness of the manor.

"We need to re-spin our auto," I say, turning slightly to give a clear view of Lera who stands next to the passenger side door. "We can pay," I say.

Still the rifle doesn't move and the door doesn't open.

"Please," I say, stepping back up onto the landing.

The barrel of the rifle pulls into the house and the door opens wider.

I slowly move into the dark foyer, and Lera joins me. After the bright snow, I can see little in the dim room, especially after the door locks thunk back into place. It's cold inside, but not as cold as outside. I back away from our host and the rifle, pushing Lera until she's partially behind me. I fight the urge to reach for my FP.

"Is Odella here?" I ask, trying to sound like I'm an old friend calling.

"Alexander Petrenko," the rifle-wielding shadow says, drawing my cover name out like a piece of bitter taffy.

"Odella?" I ask again, but I know now it's her. The voice has changed a little, gotten sharper and maybe a little deeper with age. Or maybe only a little less innocent, I'm not sure. "I–"

"You what?" But she doesn't give me a chance to answer. "I should shoot you. I could, you know. Who would hear it out here? Who would come looking for you?"

My vision has adjusted to the shadowy foyer enough to see Odella's dark shape standing against the other wall, her rifle still raised. I can't see the details of her face, however, any more than I can see the details of the room.

"You're not a killer, Odella."

"People change."

"Not like that they don't." The rifle barrel dips, and I know what I said is true, at least for her. Killing isn't part of her makeup; I don't think it ever could be, not without destroying her. The worst Odella would do is throw us out, but I can't let that happen.

"What do you want?"

"I need a spin charge," I say, hesitating for a moment before continuing, "and a place to stay for a few hours would be more than generous. I could use some sleep."

"There's a hotel in Novirsk. It's not very nice, so you should feel right at home."

Lera breaks out into a laugh. I give her a withering look, but she doesn't seem to notice.

"Circumstances make that a poor option," I say.

"That's the only reason you're here?" The tone in her voice seems to change with that question, it seems to lose some of its edge, but I'm not certain.

"Only a few hours; then the two of us will be gone."

A silence settles over the foyer, except for the click of a mantel clock in the adjacent sitting room. I'm beginning to think she is going to turn us away, when Lera steps around me.

"Please, it's only for a few hours, and then you'll never see us again," she says in what must be her most helpless voice.

Odella sighs heavily and lowers the rifle. "You can stay until tomorrow morning."

I'm about to decline, but Lera jabs me in the hip with her elbow.

Odella leads us down the hallway to the kitchen at the back of the house. There's a small fire going in the stove, giving off some heat, but not much. Using a long wood sliver, she lights the candle on the kitchen table from the handful of coal cinders in the stove.

Even with the light, I can't see Odella's face. Her hood is pulled up and a large scarf still wraps her neck and chin. She turns away to retrieve three teacups from the cupboards and sets them on the table next to a samovar.

"Sit," she says.

On the counter near the sink is a silver tray with two teacups and an assortment of tea cookies. Dishes are piled in the basin, more than one person would use in a day. The windows are covered with heavy curtains to keep out the cold, but they also keep out the light. And any prying eyes

Lera sits at the table.

I excuse myself to take care of the auto. As soon as I get free of the kitchen, the air is lighter. I draw several deep breaths, trying to ease the tension cramping my shoulders and neck muscles.

I haven't see Odella in years, and we haven't talked in longer. We didn't part under amicable terms, and

that's my fault. We had started seeing each other soon
after I finished my training with The Order. I was
eighteen, but thought I was ready to be an adult. I
met Odella at a small club around the corner from the
tiny apartment The Order issued me. She dazzled me
with her wit and intelligence and her tight dress. I told
her I was twenty-three, and made up a life partly
because I couldn't tell her what I really did but mostly
because I was arrogant–no, pompous–enough to
think I could pull it off. She told me she was twenty-
one–I learned later that she was three years older than
my constructed persona–and worked as a filing clerk
in one of the government offices. Twenty-one or
twenty-six, I wouldn't have cared because she had
nice curves, a full chest, and wanted to dote over me.

Eventually I realized that Odella wasn't what I
wanted, but I hadn't known how to break it off. After
carrying it on for a year longer than I should have, I
figured it out and ended it, but by then I had met her
parents and had even asked her to marry me,
although she should have figured out something was
wrong when I never agreed to a date. She had always
seen the best in me, until that last day. I still regret
what I did; so much so that I've never had another
relationship in the decade since.

Does she hate me? Hate is such a strong, ugly
word, but whatever her feelings about me, I earned
them.

The carriage house around back of the manor is
worn smooth and gray by the cold and wind. A few
flakes of paint flutter on window frames withered
with age. The doors resist my efforts to slide them
open, the runners corroded and needing grease, but I
manage to muscle one aside wide enough to get the

auto inside the garage. The spin-charger is nearly dead, so I stoke the generator with the last coal from a nearby bin and start to recharge the banks, then I hook the cables to the auto and open the switch. From the dials, I estimate it will take several hours to complete.

By the time I slip back into the house, I'm cold to the core again. I stand in the foyer rubbing warmth back into my arms, but I'm really delaying going back into the kitchen. Once my vision has adjusted to the gloom, I head toward the back of the house, glancing into the rooms as I go: a sitting room, a living room, a long hall that extends both to my left and right.

I stop. Ahead, Odella's voice is audible but too faint to make out what she's saying. I'm not ready to go there yet, so I turn to the left, dredging from the depths of my memory the layout of the house. Most of the doors are closed and the carpet is worn, but the third door on the left is ajar. I hear breathing, like someone asleep, but the breaths rattle as if through congested lungs.

I nudge the door open with my foot. Coals in the room's fireplace cast a faint light onto an old woman propped up on pillows in a large bed. Her face is sallow, jaw slack, and hair thinning, but it's been meticulously styled up into an intricate knot on the top of her head. Her hands twitch on her lap.

It takes me a moment to recognize Odella's mother. The years have not been kind to her. She has lost at least fifteen kilos, her cheeks now sunken and her eyes looking like they've fallen into her skull. The way the skin pulls back on her face makes her teeth look abnormally large. When I had last met her, she had been vibrant, a force to contend with as much, if not more so, than her husband. She had not liked me.

Now, looking at her, I am awash in pity.

I quietly close the door.

Feeling guilty for this invasion, I head back to the kitchen.

Lera and Odella sit at the table drinking tea and eating small sandwiches from the silver tray. They look up as I enter, but don't break their conversation.

"Mostly I take care of my mother," Odella says, her long fingers wrapped around her warm teacup. She has shed her scarf and hat. The faint light plays off the wrinkles at the corners of her eyes and around her mouth. A few gray hairs stripe her dark braid that hangs over her left shoulder. The years have worked their will on her, but even so, the beauty that first attracted me is still there. "Soon after my father died, she had a stroke. The doctors didn't think she would live, but she's a tough woman." Odella's eyes sparkle in the candlelight; she stops talking and looks down into her cup.

I'm not sure if I should sit down or leave, but I decide it would be rude to walk out at this point, and they have left a cup for me on the table. I fill the bottom of it with tea from the kettle atop the samovar and dilute it with water from the body to something that won't keep me awake, if anything could.

As I sweeten it with a dollop of jam, Odella continues, "Since then, the manor has steadily fallen apart. I don't know what needs to be done, and I couldn't keep up with it even if I did. I had hired a man to run things some years ago, but he didn't work out, and I can't afford to pay someone else because of my mother's medical bills. We have enough to live on, provided we're frugal, but nothing more."

I look around the kitchen and notice a lack of staples. That and the chill that fills every room, except for the heat from the oven and the small coal fire in her mother's room. They are living beneath frugal in a house of opulence.

The tea is hot and relaxing, a smoky blend that tickles the senses. I eat a small sandwich, and realizing how hungry I am, down another while Odella and Lera continue to talk. I don't take a third—my stomach is empty, but Odella has already given us more than she can afford.

"Sometimes I miss Aurestapol," Odella says in response to something Lera has asked. "When the days are dark and cold, like now, I sometimes get lost in the past, but the past is immutable. I can't go back. I can't change it." She looks wistfully off into the distance. "Nobody can change the past."

I am intrigued how readily Odella has opened to Lera, a total stranger who showed up on her doorstep with the man who left her a decade ago. But locked away in the shadows of this descending manor, Odella must be starved for human interaction, no matter how meager the scraps.

"Would you change the past if you could?" Lera hasn't touched her tea since I sat down at the table, her large eyes locked sympathetically upon the woman across from her

Odella blinks several times at Lera's question, as if clearing her gaze. "You *can't* change the past."

今

I SLEEP IN A BEDROOM at the end of the hall, past the room with Odella's mother and several other closed doors. Based on the dust on the armoire and tables, the room has been closed up for a long time. With the way the thick curtains are pulled, I'm surprised a skin of mildew hasn't crept up the walls, but the bed is comfortable and the blankets heavy enough to ward off the cold, and I sink into the soft mattress and a deep sleep.

When I awaken, the room is still dark. I am no longer tired, but I also don't feel entirely rested. My eyes ache, and every time I blink, something gritty scratches across them.

I light the hurricane lamp on the bedside table. The flame sputters, burning dust that stings my nose. I check my watch and hiss in surprise. Seven in the morning. I've slept nearly eighteen hours, which would explain both my grogginess and the rumble in my stomach.

I retrieve my FP from under the pillow, holster it, and pull on my suit coat then adjust it to hide the weapon.

Odella is in the kitchen, alone. The sound of me entering startles her, and she nearly cuts herself with the knife she's using to chop a beet.

"I didn't mean to—"

"It's okay," she says, sucking on her beet-stained finger. She sets the knife aside.

"I didn't expect to sleep that long," I say.

"I'm not surprised. You've had a long few days."

I am suddenly alert, my stomach pangs forgotten. Surely Lera hasn't been naive enough to tell her about St. Stephensburg. While I don't believe Odella would betray us, the less she knows, the less anyone can learn from her.

"Lera is still sleeping," Odella says. Perhaps she misread the look on my face.

"I hope she didn't keep you up late."

"No." Odella places a plate of sliced black bread on the table, along with a dish of butter. "Help yourself,"

I fill one of the teacups from the samovar and butter a slice of the bread.

Odella sits across from me, the beets forgotten on the cutting board.

I don't want to be rude after the hospitality she has given, but I don't know what else to say. After everything that happened between us all those years ago, what can I say while ignoring all that? And is "all that" a path she wants to travel down. I know I don't.

"What have you gotten yourself mixed up in, Alexander?"

Her question makes me pause in drinking my tea, and I carefully set the cup back onto its saucer. When I had gone to bed yesterday, Lera had remained at the table, but how long she and Odella had continued to talk, I don't know. Lera had slept a little in the auto, so she could have stayed awake for several hours longer than me.

"What do you mean?" I force my voice to stay calm.

A smile slides across Odella's face, one that might be reserved for an insolent toddler. "Haven't you played enough games with me, Alexander? I know what you are. I have always known."

I nearly say something, but check myself. Is she trying to coax me into revealing information? She hasn't said anything yet that proves she knows anything. It's an old interrogator's trick. If she pretends to know everything, then maybe I will let slip some piece of useful information, thinking it can't hurt because she already knows it.

Odella sighs heavily. She makes a cup of tea.

The silence, broken only by the gentle clicking of her spoon as she stirs in her jam, is palpable and heavy in the room.

I feel the overwhelming need to say something and lift the weight. "Did you ever … after me, I mean, was there anyone?"

Odella's spoon pauses. She starts to stir again and finishes by tapping the spoon on the edge of the cup and setting it aside. Shadows thrown off the hurricane lamp flicker across her face.

I had not noticed it earlier, but see now a ring on her left hand.

"Eduard," she says.

Hearing his name draws all the sound from the room. Those little noises that we hear all the time but never notice because they are always there humming away in the background. The gentle hiss of the samovar. The ticking of a far-off clock. The arctic wind against the glass of the window. The things you only notice in the world when they are gone.

"Was he a good man?"

"It depends how you define that. He was kind, as long as he avoided the drink, which he usually did. He had his share of enemies, but a man in his position often did."

"What happened?" I ask. I suspect I know. Surely if he was still around, he would be here. The fact that she still wears his ring means she did not leave him.

"The war. He enlisted when it started, feeling patriotic. He was killed a month later, somewhere on the southern front. They never said where, like it's a military secret."

"I'm sorry for your loss." The words sound hollow and inadequate, something murmured to a distant relative when you hear for the first time that her husband passed away a year ago.

"Life is about loss," she says philosophically. "Lost love, lost money, lost vitality. The longer we live, the more we lose."

This is not the Odella I knew, who had always been an optimist. She had seen the good in me, and I can't help wonder if she is like this now because of what I did to her.

"Why the frown, Alexander?"

"Hmmm?" I've been lost in my head, and she's staring at me. I take a bite of bread, buying time. The buttered rye is sweet on my tongue.

"Lera tells me you're taking her to Aurestapol."

"I am, yes," I say.

"Is she joining The Order?"

The slice of bread tumbles from my fingers and lands buttered-side down on the table.

"Don't look so surprised. And no, she did not tell me anything."

"I don't know what you're talking about."

She gives me that patronizing smile again. "I've known about The Order long before I met you, and l knew you were part of it for a long time, too. Not from the start, of course, but it wasn't difficult to put it all together. Your frequent trips, your evasive answers about what you did, and when you did answer me, you seemed to have a distinct lack of any professional knowledge—really, what sort of person in international sales would lack any basic understanding of markets?"

A deepening frown tugs at my face. I remember now the story I had told her. A horrible cover if ever there was one, but it had seemed exotic enough yet plausible at the time I had first met her.

"Your little lie didn't matter," she says, sounding almost like she's consoling me with a falsehood of her own. "What else were you to do? You couldn't exactly tell a girl you'd just met that you were a weapon of the Empire."

A weapon of the Empire? I have never been called that before. I've certainly never thought of myself that way. The Order doesn't do anything remotely weaponlike. We don't destroy or kill, except in the most desperate of situations. We nudge and cajole and manipulate, if anything, and even that might be considered a stretch.

"How did you know?" I ask.

Odella shrugs at my question, daring me to explore deeper.

I squint at her, trying to see her in a different light. Has she not been entirely honest with me either?

Before I can say anything, she laughs at me. "I'm not Order material." There's a swagger in her voice, like she's relishing having the upper hand on me. "I was a clerk in the Royal Inspector's Office, just as I told you when we first met. I assisted the inspector with a review of the activities of The Order. He compiled an impressive number of communiques."

All of this leaves me surprised, visibly I'm sure.

"It was all very quiet. I probably shouldn't even be telling you this, but it's ten years in the past now."

I try to say something but still have not completely gathered my wits.

"Why the investigation?" she asks, as if reading the words directly from my thoughts. "I was just a clerk. I was never told why, but the inspector takes orders from only one person, and only when that person is concerned about something."

As everyone knows, that one person is the emperor. No one wants the inspector looking into their business because it means nothing good. Obviously The Order has survived the investigation. I still receive my orders and move freely about the Empire, except where Krauss is concerned. Krauss. The name is bitter in my thoughts. He, too, had been in the inspector's office prior to his current position. Had he been part of this review? It might explain what he knows and might provide some basis for his misguided belief that I am not a patriot. My loyalties are firmly with The Order, and The Order is firmly with the Empire.

"Who else was involved in that review?" I ask. "Who might have seen the results, besides the emperor?"

Odella sips her tea as she considers my question. I get the sense she's trying to decide how much to tell me. "The inspector, of course."

"Of course," I reply.

"Another clerk whose name I can't recall. We seldom saw each other, and we had not met before this assignment. A tall man. Skinny, like you, only more so. Wait, I remember now. His name was Kirill. I don't think I ever learned his last name. Some of the assistant Inspectors would have been involved. Anton ... Anton–" her expression screws up as she dredges through her memories "–Anton Gorelov. Some others too, but I can't recall who now; that was long ago." She looks genuinely bothered by her failure of memory.

I thank her for telling me this, and we sit for a while longer in the flickering light. I don't know what to make of this information, and there is probably nothing to make of it. Like many things that are past, it is simply there, with no more meaning than the black bread on the plate before me.

"It's your turn to tell me something," Odella says.

The way she says this opens a pit in my stomach. She has given me something, and now I am expected the reciprocate.

"Did you ever love me?" she asks.

I don't know how to answer that because, frankly, I'm not sure I know what love is. Did I want to spend all my waking moments with her? Yes, every moment in those early days of our relationship. Did she fill a hole in my existence? Yes, she made me feel complete. Did I love her? If that is love, then I loved her, but if love is more that, than no, I didn't love her.

But I can't say that to her, when her eyes tell me that all she's looking for is a simple answer. Nothing in life is simple, however. Yet, I owe her an answer, don't I? I owe her the truth–something I've never given her.

My throat is tight as I consider what I should say.

A door opening behind Odella opens and wind and snow and white light swirl into the kitchen as someone enters from outside. I am blinded momentarily, but that doesn't stop me finding and drawing my FP and dropping to the floor.

As I peer under the table, I see the bottom of a parka and white, fur-topped boots.

"It's okay," Odella says, scraping her chair back from the table and getting between me and the parka. I'm not sure if she's talking to me or the new arrival.

I peer over the table, and see that Odella is shielding a child.

I slip the FP back into its holster. I don't think either of them saw it, so no need to scare them.

Odella steps aside. The child has drawn back the hood of her parka. She has copper skin and wavy black hair that is braided and spun into loops that hang down her back. She stares at me, her mouth hanging open in surprise.

"Alexander, this is Maya. My daughter."

I stare back at the girl, transfixed by the color of her eyes, the hard line of her jaw, and thick dark hair. They are nothing like Odella's or, I suspect, Eduard's. Yet I see Odella in the shape of the nose and the slender neck. She is Odella's child, certainly, and–it can't be, yet Maya must be ten years old or not far off.

Odella must sense the question taking form on my lips, because she speaks before I can say anything.

"This is Eduard and my daughter." She stares at me, daring me to speak, confirming my suspicions.

I lick my lips. "It's a pleasure to meet you, Maya. I am Alexander Petrenko. An old ... acquaintance of your mother's."

Maya drops in a hasty curtsy, and Odella shuffles her out of the room.

I watch the child leave, my brow pinched. The evidence is plain. I cannot pretend. "Why didn't you tell me?" I ask in a whisper, after Maya has left.

"There was nothing to tell–"

"Don't–" I stop, suddenly tongue-tied. I don't know what to say. How does one respond to finding out he has a child he never knew about. I am a father, and I never knew it, and my child–my daughter–has grown up with another man as her father.

"You're not her father," Odella says, "Eduard is."

I stagger back from her words, as if they offer a mortal blow. I grab the doorframe for support. I never knew my father because he didn't want me, and until I joined The Order, I felt that hole of rejection every day, like an abscess in my being. But Maya has never known her father because I was never told about her. My initial shock drains away. "Eduard is not her father," I hiss, fighting to keep my voice down, but not sure why. I should scream it out for all to hear, set the record straight. Yet something inside me tells me that doing so will cause more harm than good. What would I say to Maya after she knew? How could I explain why I didn't know? Odella did not tell me, sure, but some responsibility lies with me, also. I should have known. I did not.

All argument strangles in my throat. I find it hard to draw a breath, like the air has turned to bitter syrup.

Odella stares at me unsympathetically, as if I am to blame for all this. "When my mother found out I was pregnant, she arranged a quick marriage with Eduard and a long holiday carefully timed to make it look like Maya was his child, even if she bore no resemblance to him. He knew, but it didn't matter to him. I think at first it was because he would inherit this farm, all the land. Later I think he truly loved her like she was his own. After a while, not telling you was simply easier than telling you. I never expected to see you again."

I knew she would be surprised to ever see me at her door, but I never suspected this. She was so calm and collected yesterday and this morning. Maya must have been out of the house yesterday when we arrived, perhaps at school, and arrived home after I had fallen asleep. But this morning? How did she expect to keep her from me? Did she want me to find out? Did she know I would figure it out? Was this a calculated move to hurt me?

Maybe. And in some way, perhaps, I deserve it.

I don't know what Odella is capable of anymore.

The walls of the room close in around me, tightening like ice-cold chains. I want out of this place. The road calls me. Aurestapol calls me. Blissful ignorance beckons like a seductress.

Lera comes into the kitchen, wiping at her tired eyes.

"Don't sit down," I say. "It's time to go."

"But–" She sees the expression on my face and wisely doesn't argue.

At the door, Odella grabs my elbow. "I did not expect Maya home until this afternoon," she says. "I thought you would be gone by then. I didn't want you to find out like this."

"You didn't want me to find out at all."

I see the truth of my statement in her cold gaze, and it hits me like a fist. I dig the roll of money from my pocket, peel off a couple of notes, and shove them back into my pants. The rest I push into her hand.

"I don't want your money."

"Take it. If not for all of you, then for her."

"This doesn't change anything."

"I know." I leave Odella in the doorway, and Lera and I walk quickly around the manor to retrieve the auto from the carriage house. As we drive around to the front, Odella stops us in the driveway.

Lera lowers her window and Odella peers in. "You should probably know that about three weeks ago I got a visit from a man calling himself Alexei, and a tall woman with blond hair. They knew about my involvement in the investigation of The Order. They were very curious, but I don't think I told them anything they didn't already know."

I refuse to look at her, but this news surprises me no matter how calm I might appear. Alexei and Dai Lei. One is no longer a worry, but the other is still out there.

"They asked a lot questions about you, specifically, and some others."

This draws forth my surprise. Did Alexei and Dai Li know who I was in Olesk? That would explain some things, but also raises many other questions. I wonder what exactly they learned from Odella; I suspect they learned more than she thinks.

"You're full of surprises today," I say at last. I

don't think that's what Odella expected from me, but how could she expect a thank you or any other show of gratitude after what has happened this morning.

"If anyone comes asking about us, we were never here."

"I—"

"We were never here, you understand?"

She nods, her face growing pale. I want to say more, but shake my head and sigh instead. Short of telling her to leave the manor—which I doubt Odella would even consider given her mother's condition—there is nothing more I can say. Or do, at this point. Maybe when the mission is done, but by then, I suspect all the cards will have been played, and all the chips will have fallen where they may.

With a hollowness in my stomach, I engage the drive shaft and accelerate away.

今

WE COVER THE HOURS IN SILENCE. Several times
Lera looks about to speak, but thinking better of it,
stays silent. She stares out the window at the passing
plains. As we near Aurestapol, the snow disappears,
replaced by fallow, muddy fields and heavy gray
clouds that threaten rain. The day has warmed too
much for it to snow, but it's still cold, and a damp
wind bites to the bone as we wait impatiently in the
gloom for our auto to spin-charge one last time.

The somber fields gradually give way to buildings,
a few at first and then progressively more, growing in
size and height. We cross the Sten River and enter
Aurestapol proper.

The closeness of the old buildings comforts me,
and my fingers ease up on the steering wheel. I am
surprised how much they ache, and I realize I have
been squeezing the steering wheel tightly all day. It's
late afternoon, just after closing time for most
businesses, but the crowds have already gone home.
Only a few people are left pushing their way through
the wind.

I turn from street to street without really thinking about where I'm going. I don't need to think—I don't want to—my body knows where to go on its own. Eventually I curb the auto in front of a two-story stone building with rows of little rectangular windows. The stone is stained black from decades of coal soot.

Leaning forward, I look up at the corner window on the top floor. It's dark, whereas several of the others glow softly.

"What is this place?" Lera asks.

"We call it seven-Orion. It's one of our safe houses."

She follows me up the wooden stairs to the top floor where the smell of roasted pork is heavy in the hallway. We stop at the end door, and I check to make sure no one is watching. Seeing no one, I pry the edge of the wainscoting away and a key drops into my hand.

We go inside, and I chain the door behind us.

Lera wanders through the single room, dragging her fingers across the back of the old sofa, along the dials of the console radio, over the face of the wooden mantel clock, ticking away the present.

"Stay away from the windows," I say, checking to make sure the blackout curtains are pulled closed.

On the wall in the kitchen is a phone. I lift the handset and dial R's extension, watching the rotary spin back between each number. It seems to move very slowly. I wait, a slight static filling the line. After what seems like a full minute, the line clicks as a connection is made. R's extension buzzes. Once. Twice. My rising panic is dispelled when she picks up.

"Speak to me." There is a palpable tension in R's

voice, but every time I have called her on her extension, she sounds the same, and I assume it is because only serious calls are made to this number.

"Calypto," I say, not wasting time or words. "I'm here."

R sighs loudly, an exhalation that crackles through the speaker. "You're late."

I didn't expect her to say anything else. If I'm calling, I must be all right. If I don't call, then I'm dead, and she has other things to worry about.

"I ran into train trouble." When she doesn't stop me, I continue, "I think this is related to the recent assassination."

"Let's discuss it later," she says. "Meet me at the fountain in Korelov Park in one hour. Do you know the place?"

I tell her I do. "Wait," I say before she can hang up. I'm not sure how to broach the matter that is bothering me, so I decide to go at it head on. "Why didn't you tell me I was bringing in a recruit?"

The line crackles in R's silence. After an uncomfortably long pause, she says, "At the time, I didn't know."

"How–"

"This isn't the time, Calypto. We can debrief later."

"Wait," I say again, but the phone clicks and the line goes quiet. I stare at the handset, not sure I heard her right. How could she not know that the Class-A she sent me for was a person? A miscommunication must have happened somewhere up the chain; that's the type of error that can get someone killed. In this business, surprises are rarely fun.

I place the handset back into its cradle. I don't have time to worry about that now. Korelov Park is at least a half-hour walk from the safe house. It's in the city center, not far from the White Palace, so we can't take the auto. Vehicles aren't allowed in that area.

In the closet by the door, I find several coats and hats in various sizes and styles for both men and women. I pull out one I think will fit Lera. It's not the latest style, but it looks warm. "Time to go," I say.

She gives me back my long coat, and I pull it on. The inside is still warm with her body heat.

When we reach the street, Lera pulls up at the doorjamb. Even though night is still an hour off, the sky is already black and gloomy with ominous clouds; the air is heavy, and it feels like it will rain any minute.

"We've got to go," I say, pulling gently on her arm.

She pulls back against me.

"If we don't hurry, we *will* get caught in the rain. You can do this."

She swallows hard enough for me to hear it, and to her credit she comes.

We turn right and head toward city center, walking at a purposeful pace, but one that I hope doesn't look rushed. Even so, Lera is nearly running to keep pace.

I force myself to slow down. It's probably better to move with more measured caution anyways. Walking as fast as I was, I could miss something important. I scan the streets ahead, and frequently look behind for signs of anyone lying in wait or following us. Only a few middle-aged men in long gray coats scuttle along in the closing gloom. I see no signs of anyone taking interest in us.

We wind our way through the narrow streets of Old Aurestapol, and reach the southern edge of Korelov Park as night is settling over the city. We pause at the iron archway leading into the park. A pebbled path passes under it and disappears into the trees.

Korelov Park was built sixty years ago for the World's Fair and is one of Aurestapol's beloved landmarks. It's a haven of green in the otherwise stone and metal of a large industrial city, but it also forms a symbolic center for the Empire. The White Palace, official home of the emperor, sits on its northern boundary. On the east is the Ministry building, where the lords meet to execute governance, and to the west is Aurestapol's great library building. The south end of the park opens into an old neighborhood that at one time housed prominent citizens, but has since fallen into disrepair. Korelov Park is at the center of learning, governance, the people and the emperor.

I hesitate at the iron archway. With the recent curfew, no one goes into the park at night anymore. The blackout curtains on the windows of the nearby buildings are pulled closed, so the buildings are solid bricks of shadow in the fading light.

I squint through the archway, but my vision doesn't pierce far into the blackness. I don't like this at all, and I wonder what R was thinking in selecting this location to meet.

"We're not going in there," Lera says, a slight tremble in her voice.

I draw my FP and slip it into the pocket of my long coat, where it will be easier to reach. I click on my hand torch while shielding the light with my body so no will see it. Confident it is working, I turn it off so it won't spoil my night sight, but I hold it ready in my hand. After one more check of the street, I step through the iron archway.

Lera stays on the outside, hugging herself. Her eyes seem to glow in the failing daylight.

"It's not far," I say. "Then you'll be safely onto the next stage of your life." I try to sound calm, but too much can still happen. Yet it's more than that. She is still innocent, and she needs someone to look after her. Even as I think this, I know it's foolish. She is capable; otherwise she would not have made it out of the orphanage. And over the next months, The Order will train her to be even more capable. Deadly capable.

Yet something about that seems wrong.

Lera passes under the arch and takes my hand. Her fingers are warm, and their heat radiates up my arm.

Reluctantly, I pull my fingers free. "I might need them," I say.

We turn toward the dark trees. The fountain is at the center of the park, a short walk from here. The gravel trail crunches under my shoes, and narrow evergreens shush in the damp wind. Above, naked branches clatter like wooden chimes.

The trail twists through the trees, a line just a shade lighter than the darkness so I can follow it. After a short distance, the trees part, and a glossy black surface spreads out before us: Korelov Lake. The trail forks, and we go left, hugging the curving shoreline.

A narrow strip of scraggly grass separates us from the dark wall of trees. While the trees block us from view of the street and the buildings along the edge of the park, anyone could be hiding in them, and I'd never see them.

I reach into my pocket and grip the handle of my

FP.

Ahead the white stones of Korolev Fountain reflect the last of the day's gray light. The fountain is a series of stone pillars and waist-high blocks laid out in three concentric circles. At the center is a geodesic sphere made of bronzed beams. When the fountain was operational, jets of water rose and fell in the middle of the sphere and colored lights would turn the pulsing cascades red and blue and green. It was the height of technology the year it was built, and it was the centerpiece of that year's World's Fair and the pride of the Empire in the years since. But with the war and the shortages, the fountain has been neglected and fallen into disrepair.

Against the white stones, a stout shadow paces back and forth. From the shape, it can only be R.

I release a relieved breath that mists faintly in the cold evening air, and quicken my stride. Lera, moving quickly, stays at my side.

As we near, R turns suddenly on me, a pistol in her hand.

Lera yelps.

"It's Calypto," I whisper quickly.

R flashes a small penlight into my face, blinding me momentarily, then clicks it off. "Were you followed?"

Usually she complains about my tardiness.

"No," I say. "Who do you expect might be following us?" I hope I can get some information, but R doesn't bite at the bait—not that I really expected her to.

R doesn't lower her pistol. "Let me see you, girl." She steps closer and clicks on her penlight again. "Quite extraordinary," she whispers, like an art connoisseur might upon seeing a masterwork for the first time. "If half of what they say about your sight is true ..."

Lera lowers her face and turns away, hiding slightly behind my shoulder. Intimidated no doubt, but then, everything about R can be intimidating.

"You did well, Calypto. I will take it from here."

"I have news."

"Now is not the best time." The intensity in her voice tells me not to argue, but this conversation cannot wait.

"The mark I showed you at the Grand Station, it's a Quin symbol–"

"It means nothing to me."

Her rapid, forceful denial doesn't feel genuine. R knows more than I do about most everything; it comes with her position. I don't expect her to tell me all she knows, but .... "I need to know–"

"I'll tell you what you need to know."

"You know what that symbol means. You know who they are."

R doesn't say anything, and in doing so she confirms my suspicions. I have always trusted R; she has never given me a reason not to. She has always had my back. As much as I may disagree, she believes there is a reason I don't need to know.

"I met others with that mark," I say. "Some of them tried to kill me, so I think I–" how do I put it? "–I deserve to know what I'm up against."

R shows no sign that what I've said has registered.

Maybe "deserve" isn't the right word. "Deserve" suggests entitlement, and I've never been entitled to anything, especially not from The Order. Nothing in The Order has ever been handed to me. "I've *earned* an answer."

R's shoulders rise and fall as she exhales a cloud of mist. "I was afraid of this." In the darkness, her face is a formless shadow, but I imagine her lips pressing into a thin line as she contemplates exactly what to say. And what not to.

"I have not been told anything, at least nothing officially, but I have heard about this group from some other field ops. I've quietly asked questions, but I've not gotten anywhere. I haven't been stonewalled; I've just not received any satisfactory answers, and I'm not sure those answers exist. They do not appear to be a large group, and there is much hearsay right now. I don't know enough to piece it together."

"The assassination…."

"Yes. Based on what you saw, they were responsible for that, even if official word is that it was a Papalate spy."

"Are they allied with the Papalate?"

"I don't know," R says, displeasure obvious in her tone. To admit she doesn't know must be difficult for her. She is always in control. Whenever I'm with her, she is the smartest person in the room. "Anything that weakens us, favors our enemy."

"They've been asking questions about The Order," I say. "Why aren't we doing anything about them?"

"That is a large leap for one with a limited view, but I understand your perspective," R says, her annoyance plain. "Like you, I must trust those above me in the chain. We all have our orders. These are not things for you to be concerned about right now, however. Go home, Calypto; you have earned a vacation."

I have earned one. I want to curl under a thick

blanket and sleep until spring. Well, maybe not that long, but at least well into tomorrow. I want a good meal, too, but still, this whole thing eats at me. "One more—"

"Not now."

"Just—"

"No more."

But I won't be put off. Tonight I want only one more answer, if there is an answer to be had. "Who is Alexander Olstevski?"

"Where did you hear that name?" The sharpness in her voice makes me step back.

"Who is he?"

"Forget that name," R says. "For your own good, don't speak it again, and this conversation is over." R turns away, as if to punctuate she is done talking, but then turns back to me. "I want you on the next train to Tanev," she says, raising a silencing finger before I can protest. "You're to enjoy the sun and find some company. I don't want to see or hear from you for at least two weeks."

"But—"

"That's an order." R seizes Lera's arm and starts away. I have never seen R respond like this before. She sounds genuinely upset, verging on scared.

"Who is he?" I ask her back, but she doesn't answer. "Tell—"

A cold sensation ripples down my spine, and the world around me stutters as reality comes out of alignment. I dive forward, knocking R and Lera apart and to the ground. Fragments of red hot metal sting my cheek as dozens of flechettes splinter on the stones. I keep rolling away until I hit the base of a column.

Lera lies on the ground covering her head with one arm. With her other hand she gropes on the ground around her, and I realize her goggles have been knocked off. Her whimpers reach me through the gloom.

A body length away from Lera, R's dark shape lies splayed on the ground, motionless.

"Lera," I whisper hoarsely. "Don't move." But she doesn't hear me, and continues to search for her goggles. Exposed as she is, she's an easy target. "I'm coming to get you."

I dart out and grab her wrist. My back strains under her weight, but she's up, half-running, half-dragged by me. Flechettes whistle from two, maybe three different directions, sparking off nearby columns. We tumble behind a waist-high stone block. Flechettes splinter the ground, slice through my trouser leg, burning like wasp stings as they cut into my thigh above my knee.

I clench my teeth, biting off a scream. I can't let Lera know I've been hit.

I press my back against the block, trying to flatten myself into the stone. There is more than one attacker, but in the commotion of the ambush, I'm not sure how many or where they are hiding.

I tighten my grip on my FP and strain to hear anything through the heavy darkness, but it's fallen so quiet; they could have magically vanished entirely. I'm afraid to move, afraid to breathe, because they must still be out there.

Lera presses against me. Her breathing is machine gun fast, and I fear she will black out if she can't get it under control. I squeeze her arm, trying to reassure her. She stares forward, her eyes milky white in the night.

There is just enough light to see shadows on darkness and the faint outline of the marble columns and blocks. R still hasn't moved, and at this distance, I can't tell if she's breathing. It's too dark to see if she's bleeding. I can only pray that her wound, whatever it is, is not serious, and that she's playing dead so as not to attract more harm while she waits for an opportunity to help.

I lean toward the edge of the stone block, and bite off a gasp of pain, but not before some of it escapes. White-hot sparks cloud my vision like angry fireflies.

My trouser leg is wet and my hand comes away sticky. Clean holes puncture the front and back of my thigh where the flechettes passed through the muscle, missing the bone and the femoral artery. I can still move if I have to, but I'll likely need stitches to close the wounds properly.

"We have to get out of here," I whisper. Lera doesn't answer. She continues to stare into the darkness, seemingly overwhelmed by what's happened.

I grab her chin, intending to turn her face to mine and hopefully bring her focus back to the here and now, but she slaps at my hand and tries to crawl away. I lunge at her and pull her back behind the cover of the stone block. "Lera!" I say several times, until she stops thrashing against me.

"Listen to me," I say. "If we can get to the trees, we have a chance." My heart thumps hard. Such a move will either catch them by surprise or get us killed. Peering around the corner of the block, I see nothing across the fountain's jumble of stones and columns. They're out there, but I have no idea where.

For all I know, I'm about to send us to our deaths, but if we stay where we are, they are certain to kill us.

"About ten meters directly in front of you is another stone block."

"I can't see it." Lera's voice is tense, desperate. "I can't see anything!"

"That doesn't matter. We're going together." I squeeze her right hand with my left.

"I can't do this. I can't." Her panic is rising again.

"Don't think; just do," I say. "Stay low. Move fast. On three. One … two …" I stop counting because something is wrong—or maybe I simply lose my nerve—but Lera was anticipating my "three" and she starts to move. I stutter an incomprehensible protest, but she's already rising up from her crouch. I squeeze her hand, but feel her fingers slipping free. I hold her just long enough to stop her from getting fully to her feet. Off balance, she stumbles and falls to the ground with a surprised cry as flechettes whistle through the air where we would have been if we had moved as planned. I pull her back to cover as more flechettes whiz from a different angle through the darkness, sparking off the stone. I'm tempted to return fire, but I can't afford to waste my ammunition shooting blindly into the dark. I have no extra cartridges.

Lera pants heavily while she shakes violently.

"You're okay," I say, trying to calm her.

She holds her left hand delicately in her lap. The palm is scraped from her fall. "Why didn't you go?" she asks.

"Change of plans," I say.

"What's the new plan?" She flinches as flechettes whistle overhead. They know where we are now, and they're keeping us pinned down with sporadic fire. Likely one of them is flanking us, trying to get a clear shot.

I check the ammunition on my FP. I have four, maybe five bursts left, and I need to save one just in case … My fingers tremble as I snap the cartridge back into place. I'm still on my mission, I think grimly, and I can't let a Class-A fall into enemy hands.

"What's your plan?" Lera asks again.

I don't want to admit I don't have one.

Flechettes ricochet off the rock.

If only I knew how many attackers and where they were, we might have a chance.

A drop of icy water splashes on my head. Another strikes the stone next to my hand. In the next second, the clouds open and the rain falls in heavy sheets of slush.

Lera screams and covers her head with her jacket while trying to burrow behind me for cover, but she has nowhere to go. She tries to run again, but I grab her before she can expose herself, and I hug her to me. She thrashes in my arms, shrieking like the raindrops are acid, not water.

The sound tears at me, and I realize the rain is worse than any acid. In the snows of St. Stephensburg, she was nearly incapacitated by what she saw, what she felt. In the rain of Aurestapol she would be overwhelmed. I can't begin to understand what it would be like to see every person in the Empire's largest and most populous city – no, not just to see them, but to see *into* them, to feel every person's pain and fear, especially in these desperate times.

Every person … including those hunting us.

Fire in the Snow

She can be my eyes.

"Lera," I say, as gently as possible. Our time is running out—the rain has bought us a momentary reprieve—and it's hard to keep the desperation from my voice. She shivers in my arms. "I need you to open your eyes and tell me where they are."

"No!"

Her talent has hurt her in the past. I saw what it could do to her in the snows of St. Stephensburg, and with what I am asking, I could be sentencing her to a fate worse than death. But if she doesn't at least try....

I have killed, and regretted nearly every death, but those deaths were always an enemy that wished to do me harm. Lera wishes me no harm; in truth, she expects me to protect her, and that's what I will do. Right up to the moment when I can no longer do that. Then, for the good of the Empire, I cannot let her fall into the hands of those who would do this country harm.

"I can't do this without you," I say. I want to tell her everything will be okay, but my voice cracks.

We are almost out of time. I feel it in my bones, in the shiver down my spine. Our attackers will have angles on us soon.

My fingers tighten on the grip of my FP. A burst under her chin and up into her head would be quickest.

The lump in my throat hurts as I slowly turn the pistol tip toward her.

I will give her until the count of three.

"Open your eyes, Lera; I can't do his alone."

The numbers begin to tick off in my head.

One.

The number that people view as triumphant, but really represents the loss of everything meaningful. Victory comes not from vanquishing everyone else.

Two.

The number of chances everyone deserves, because we all disappoint at some time. I got my second chance when The Order found me. Everyone deserves a second chance, especially Lera.

Thr–

"I'll do it," Lera says, her voice barely a whisper.

The tension in my body suddenly releases. My finger eases, and the trigger settles back into place.

Lera slides from my arms into the puddle that has formed under us. The icy water flows over her hands as she lowers her face into it.

Her body immediately tenses, and for a second I want to yell at her to close her eyes, but I fight off the urge by blowing on my hand, trying to get feeling back into my trigger finger. I won't get more than one shot at each of our assailants. Otherwise, I am completely still, fearing that any movement will disrupt Lera. I count the seconds in my head, purposely slow seconds because I think those are right. Time has a habit of moving faster in my head than in reality. Or maybe I just want time to move slower, to give us more of it.

I hear something through the falling raindrops to my left and swing my pistol in that direction. Through the dark and the downpour, I see nothing, but I'm still alive so I must be hearing things.

Lera raises her head, her held breath exploding from her lungs. "Ten meters over there," she says pointing just to the right of where I thought I heard the sound. "Fifteen meters over there." Her arm swings to the other side of us.

A shadow that I never would have seen creeps slowly between two columns. I swing my FP around and fire a burst that whistles over top of Lera's prone body. As that shadow drops, I bring the weapon back around to where Lera first pointed, an area of darkness backed by trees. It's too dark, the rain too heavy, but he's there. I need to trust that he is there, ten meters away. I fire, the compressed gas puffing a soft staccato barely audible above the pounding rain. A surprised scream from the darkness. A second later, a dull thud and a splash as our attacker drops into a puddle.

Lera's face is back in the black water, her body convulsing now as if she's having a seizure. Her arms flail out at to the side, and the weight of her crouching body must be driving her face into the stone. Air gurgles through the water; she'll drown if she inhales.

I reach down to lift her head, but it snaps up on its own, and she topples over onto her back. Her eyes are wide and wild.

She screams.

Her agony is shrapnel cutting painfully into my flesh, stabbing into my head. I grab my temples.

Lera curls into a ball, still screaming, but her wail slowly loses its power, and extends as if someone is pulling out every last bit of breath and pain with a grappling hook and rope. Her entire body is tense, every muscle taut like wire cables.

What have I done?

I squeeze her to me, trying to quell her shaking, but I cannot stop it. Her eyelids flutter rapidly, as if her eyes have rolled back into her head, but they are all white, and I can't tell. She's no longer screaming; her only sound is now a ragged whimper.

"You did it," I whisper, rocking her gently. I can barely speak my throat is so tight. "We're safe."

"No," she says. Her mouth is close to me, yet I can barely hear her because the word is so insubstantial. "One … more …." Her hand twitches, her finger pointing vaguely toward my chest.

It takes me a second to realize she isn't pointing at me, but through me, and through the stone block we lean against.

My body jerks straight. I try to draw a breath, but I cannot force air into my lungs. The rain eases, but the sound of the slushy drops splattering on my head is loud.

He's back there, coming around or over the stone block, but which way I don't know.

I close my eyes; they're useless in the rain and the dark anyway. I try to calm myself, but the tension in my muscles only increases.

Then it comes, a second of vertigo that wrenches my stomach and twangs the muscles in my back. My eyes shoot open, the world around me frozen for a split second. Raindrops hang suspended in the air like diamonds in oil. From the corner of my eye, I see nothing between the drops to my left. I swing my FP to the right as the world jumps forward and the raindrops fall on me like a deluge.

I fire. Flechettes whistle from the barrel of my pistol, striking the dark shadow that has just appeared around the edge of the stone.

The first burst staggers him, giving me a cleaner shot.

The second burst drops him.

Thankfully, I don't need a third because the cartridge is empty.

I have no strength left. My arm drops to my side; my FP clatters onto the ground.

The rain eases and then stops. A fine mist persists, hanging in the air like a winter breath.

"It's all over," I say, but Lera doesn't answer.

She clutches me, shaking uncontrollably, soaked through to the skin. I pull her against me, trying to share my warmth, but she isn't shaking from the cold. All those lives out there, all those souls she peered into, like a voyeur of the damned. All that emotion experienced in one monumental flood. What has it done to her?

What have I done to her? My life for hers; that's what I've done, and a damn poor trade it is.

LERA DRIFTS AWAY, like a leaf blown across Korolov Lake. Her shaking grows less, until it's a shiver, and then a slight tremble, and then nothing. She goes limp in my arms, but her shoulders still rise and fall with a gentle rhythm of breath. I hope she has fallen asleep and not into something worse, but I have no way to know.

I LIFT LERA FROM THE PUDDLE and lay her on the stone block. Her limbs fall akimbo, all unnatural angles. Gently I move them back to her sides. Her fingers are ice cold.

My leg aches as I bend to collect my assailant's weapon, but against the background of a greater pain, it is inconsequential. My attacker lies nearby, his square face up, his unblinking eyes white in the darkness. Water droplets dot his fuzzy hair like stars.

I know him from the streets of St. Stephensburg. I know the mark that must surely stain the back of his neck.

I check the other two. Both are dead, having bled out from their wounds.

To my surprise, R is alive. With her penlight, I examine the wound in her shoulder. She was fortunate the flechettes missed the arteries in her neck. She has a large knot on her forehead where she struck the stones when she fell. I tear away a piece of my shirt, and as I push it against her wound, she stirs.

"Don't move," I say.

She blinks at me, her mind slightly foggy, I suspect. "Lera?" she croaks.

"She's alive …." I can't bring myself to say anything more.

"That's what's important."

I don't know about that. I've learned that for some there are things worse than death. For Lera, one of those things might very well be The Order. They will give her a new life, certainly, a chance at a new future, but that new future will come at a price. They want her because of her talent, and they will require her to use it.

R grabs my wrist again. "We need to get her to safety." She sits up with a grunt. "Help me."

"You should–"

"Shut up and help me."

R is a tough woman. Her wound would incapacitate most men.

I pull her to her feet. She draws a sharp breath and grimaces.

"You're injured," she says, noticing that I have most of my weight on my left leg.

"Passed clean through," I say, trying to sound unconcerned. I've endured worse, but the wound still hurts. "I'll make it."

"Can you carry her?"

"I can."

R leans over the body of the fuzzy-haired attacker. In the narrow beam of the penlight his open, lifeless eyes sparkle. The puddle in which he lies shimmers like a ruby.

"He's one of them," I say. "A Silver Tiger."

R nods, but I'm not sure if it's in understanding or confirmation.

"There's two more of them," I say. "Both dead."

R shakes her head, and I can hear her disappointment in my own: we'll get no information from them.

"One of us was followed." I don't say anything more, but I'm pretty sure I wasn't. That thought sends a chill through me that's colder than the damp wind off the lake. If R had been followed, then the Silver Tigers had infiltrated The Order deeper and for longer than I ever imagined. But to what purpose?

I suspect R realizes this too, but she gives me no indication. She winces as she straightens from examining the dead man and turns to me, cradling her right arm in her left. "It's time to go."

"Give me a moment," I say as I scan the dark ground until I find Lera's goggles. I scoop water into them from a puddle and gently put them back on her face. Her eyes don't open, but her lips move slightly, and she makes a faint sound. I'm sure that they aren't actually words, but I imagine she says, "You're not an ass." A trick of my mind, most certainly, but it makes me feel better nonetheless.

"She needs a doctor," I say as I slip my arms under her shoulders and knees. With a grunt, I lift her and roll her weight in toward my chest.

"You did well, Calypto."

Ordinarily, this high praise from R would leave me elated, but not today. Somehow, I feel I have failed, but then I remind myself what every field agent knows: if you come home with the world in no worse a state, then you've done a good job. And you know what? Lera *will* be better off in The Order. They will teach her to harness her power and use it for the good of the Empire because that's what The Order does.

These words, however, sound like a pep talk in my head, like a mantra to convince away my doubts. I can't help feeling the world is in a worse state today than it was before I left for Olesk.

We head out of the park, R in the lead, me following behind. My leg protests, but I ignore it. Lera is surprisingly heavy for such a wisp of a girl, but that simply means there is more to her than meets the eye.

But that, I already know.

End of Book One

Thank you for reading Book One of the Calypto Cycle. Gaining exposure as an independent author relies mostly on word-of-mouth, so if you have the time and inclination, please consider leaving a short review wherever you can.

MEET THE AUTHOR

D. Thomas Minton writes from his home in the Pacific Northwest of the United States, where he lives a short walk from vineyards and alpaca farms. When not writing, he travels to remote locations and helps communities across the Pacific Ocean protect coral reefs. His stories have appeared in some of science fiction's top publications. He can found online at dthomasminton.com.

A sneak peek at
Shackles of Doubt
Book Two of the Calypto Cycle

ALMOST GETTING KILLED makes people think you need time off to recover, but I've waltzed with death before; she's no strange dance partner. This is more about getting me out of the way, I think, so I can't ask questions. In Tanev, my questions fester like an open wound. I don't like having so much time to think. Thinking is an operative's most hazardous activity.

My shadow's shoes pad softly behind me, quieter today than they were last night, but probably he is being more cautious because the streets are empty this afternoon, except for the two of us.

Tanev has cobblestone streets with narrow sidewalks and buildings that look individually hand-built instead of die-cast like the Empire's more recent, industrial towns. Nearly as old as Aurestapol, Tanev dates back to before the Emperor's line ascended to the White Throne. It was built as a playground for the noble families, and many of the buildings look like those you'd find in the more reputable neighborhoods of Aurestapol proper, only in miniature and with rustic trappings in the wooden accents and crafted wrought iron fixtures. Autos aren't allowed in the city center, so the place feels like I've stepped through a doorway to a hundred years ago.

Ahead, sitting on a stoop, a man in a white shirt watches my approach. As I near he rises and flashes something in his hand: a cigarette tucked between his fingers.

"Spare a light?" he asks. He motions again with his cigarette hand. Nestled in his palm is a matchbook such that only I can see it.

"Sure, sure," I say, patting my pockets. He's caught me off guard, and I fumble for a little time while I study his clean-shaven face. I've not seen him before; he's very young, a fresh recruit into whatever scheme he's working today. He's barely legal age I would guess, but he's playing his part with a calm that suggests more experience than his baby-face implies.

I have no matches. I don't smoke, but I pretend to draw out a matchbook. My fumbling around gives the man time to move his cigarette to lips where he leaves it dangling. As we make the mock transfer, he flips the matchbook from his palm into his fingers and holds it up, like a magician completing his illusion. Anyone watching would be convinced I gave it to him. He tears away a match and scrapes it across the back of the book. The match flares brightly, smelling of sulfur. Bluish smoke trails from the corner of his mouth. The cigarette tip glows like a fanned ember. He exhales to the side so as not to blow smoke into my face.

"I needed that," he says with a smile. I can't immediately place his accent, not that it matters because I doubt it's his true manner of speech. He hands the matchbook to me, and I stuff it into my pocket without looking at it. "Thank you." He motions with the cigarette as if he needs to explain his gratitude; then he sits down again and takes pleasure in his smoke.

I continue on my way.

Several blocks later, I notice my shadow again. Likely he circled around to avoid walking past the cigarette man. Maybe he's not as much an amateur as I originally thought. If he's no amateur, maybe he wants me to know I'm being watched, which I suspect is something a Red Cuff would do, thinking his presence would unsettle his target. For ordinary people that might be true, and as the thought occurs to me now, it does put more of a knot in my stomach than usual, but nothing that would ever give me pause.

I reach my guest house and return to my room. It's nothing fancy–a square room slightly larger than that to which I am accustomed, a firm bed with stiff sheets, and a chair in the corner that catches the morning sun through the room's only window. The window looks out onto a small courtyard with vine-covered trellises and a pair of benches. I've not been down to it.

I lock the door, and pull the curtains shut. They're sheer and let enough light into the room, but keep out prying eyes.

I fish the matchbook from my pocket. Printed on the cover is a cat in a top hat and bow tie. In yellow script is the name "Club Hat Cat." A stupid name for a club, but I've seen it in my wanderings–a small place in a walk-down a short distance from my room. Written inside the cover is the number 1830, which I assume is a time. The handwriting is sloppy, as if someone took care to make sure it could not be easily traced back to its author. I peel the matches back looking for more information, but find nothing. Satisfied there is no more to learn, I tear free a match and set the book on fire, turning it carefully to ensure that it is entirely consumed. Before it burns my fingers, I drop it into the toilet. It sizzles as it goes out leaving a spreading puddle of ash on the surface of the water. I flush it down.

I crack open the window to let out the smell of the burned match book.

I check my pocket watch, and snap it closed. It's early still. I have nothing to do but wait. And think.

Look for
Shackle of Doubt, Book Two of the Calypto Cycle
at an online vendor near you in 2017.

www.ingramcontent.com/pod-product-compliance
Lightning Source LLC
Chambersburg PA
CBHW021044130626

46552CB00005B/2012